LOST AND FOUND

Look for other REMNANTS™
titles by K.A. Applegate:

#1 The Mayflower Project

#2 Destination Unknown

#3 Them

#4 Nowhere Land

#5 Mutation

#6 Breakdown

#7 Isolation

#8 Mother May I?

#9 No Place Like Home

Also by K.A. Applegate:

ANIMORPHS ®

REMNANTS™

LOST AND FOUND

K.A. APPLEGATE

AN
APPLE
PAPERBACK

SCHOLASTIC INC.
New York Toronto London Auckland Sydney
Mexico City New Delhi Hong Kong Buenos Aires

ISBN 0-590-88494-8

12 11 10 9 8 7 6 5 4 3 2 1   3 4 5 6 7 8/0

Printed in the U.S.A.   40
First printing, January 2003

For Michael and Jake

CHAPTER ONE

THERE WAS NO MORE "UTOPIA."

Month Three

Jobs was on watch. As usual, he'd volunteered for the second watch because lately he hadn't been able to sleep more than a few hours a night. What did it matter if he had to get out of bed at midnight if he was awake anyway?

It had been approximately ninety days since Billy had saved them all — barely — by erecting a sort of fortress a bit more than the height and breadth of the ship's elevator and the rooms on top — the attic, as the Remnants called it, and the lab. Ninety days and ninety nights, three months now, of fighting off the Blue Meanies and the Riders, both of whom the Remnants had insulted by breaking the Big Compromise and turning Mother toward Earth. Ninety days and ninety nights of living under seige. Of desperate guerrilla attacks, of endless vigilance.

Jobs was more tired than he'd ever been. But

they were still in control of Mother but anything could change that. Anything.

Charlie, who'd wandered into *Billyville* and then betrayed them, had run off. Back to Amelia and the third member of what Billy, Jobs, and the others were now calling the Troika. It was a name Billy thought suited highly evolved and mutated humans. He didn't explain why. Not yet anyway. This was shortly after the horrible battle in which Charlie had mutated into a hideous, lethal porcupinelike creature and tried to use 2Face to get to Billy. It was the battle in which Kubrick had been killed while trying to save 2Face's life. Now Billy had gotten a message from Amelia, Charlie, and a guy named Duncan Choate. The message had come via a low-level Blue Meanie. The Remnants let the Meanie into the fortress to deliver a short speech in words scrolled across his suit's chest screen and in Meanie sign language.

The message was simple: Amelia, Charlie, and Duncan were *not* happy. Their attempt to destroy Billy had failed. So, they declared themselves enemies and once again ordered Billy to return the ship to its original course.

Billy and the other Remnants — via a strongly worded reply by 2Face — refused. The Meanie had been sent back to the Troika with the message. Things were not good — to say the least.

There was no more "utopia." And for that one thing Jobs was glad. It had all seemed wrong from the very beginning. So wrong Jobs had been obsessed with the hunt for Earth or some other habitable planet. A place where the remnants of the human species could — possibly — rebuild. Maybe just live out the rest of their lives in some sort of peace. And freedom.

Because even though the Remnants were technically "free," Jobs felt as though they were prisoners of war. How free could anyone really be aboard the supership of an alien species? How free could you be when every time you stepped outside the fortress you had to carry a weapon and still run the risk of being ambushed and worse?

All Jobs wanted to do — all anyone wanted to do at this point — was get the ship to Earth safely and without the further loss of life. No one really spoke about what would happen after they got there.

Jobs looked out at what had been the field of battle. The ship's — Mother's — default environment and the Riders' natural habitat. It was a swampy place, with copper-colored water, silty mud, high yellow grasses, and strange, superbendy trees.

Riders and Meanies. The Squids — though they were all gone now — and the Remnants. And Charlie Langlow, Amelia, and Duncan Choate, whatever they were. Too many groups all trying to control one ship. Life on board Mother had been a fight from the very beginning.

Jobs heard a low chime coming from Mother's attic.

Six A.M. Six hours after Jobs had gone on duty. Six A.M. ship time. There was no "time" here on Mother, not in the way the humans had worked it out back on Earth. Time, space, time-space . . . Jobs thought a lot about these things now, about Mother tunneling through wormholes.

"Hey, Duck. Relief is here."

It was Mo'Steel. Jobs smiled. No matter what, the sight of his best friend wildly grinning made Jobs happy.

"Everything's pretty quiet," Jobs said.

Mo'Steel grinned even wider and shifted his crossbow from one hand to the other. "So, we're bunnying out, huh? I was hoping for some action."

"No. Really?" Jobs said, smiling as he walked off toward the elevator's ascending platform, which would take him to his bed.

CHAPTER TWO

LIFE IN A BUBBLE.

Violet was just off guard duty. She took the elevator up to the attic, stepped off, looked around. This alien decor was a far cry from the beautiful Mediterranean villa Billy had created for her.

But Violet never actually missed her villa. At first she thought she might. It had been gorgeous, a lovely refuge. False, though, and lonely. The place where she'd been attacked by a Meanie. And the place where Roger Dodger had hurt himself playing with a Rider boomerang. Where she'd saved his life by using the worms that were now a part of her. Where she'd discovered her own personal mutation.

So there were plenty of reasons for Violet not to care about losing the villa. The fortress was a utilitarian space. It did its job.

Violet passed through one of the massive arches that opened off the attic's foyer, walked slowly down a long, long hallway. Everything in the attic was gigantic in proportion.

The fortress itself encompassed the ship's elevator from basement to attic. The outer walls were comprised of shields that allowed the Remnants to see out without allowing enemies to see in. A mere brush against the outside of the shield would produce an electric shock. Billy and Jobs spent a lot of time perfecting the shields.

Life in a bubble.

The Remnants now occupied the large quarters surrounding the bridge, rooms built by the Shipwrights a long time ago. How long ago no one knew. The living there was simple. Since there really wasn't enough protected room in the attic for everyone to have their own space, they set up an area for the females, another for the males. They designated a common dining area, like a cafeteria. Jobs's lab was in the attic, too.

Billy was pretty much always on the bridge. He'd reverted to that hollow-eyed, superpale, refugee, orphan look.

2Face was still recovering from her wounds and had a bed in the dorm, though Violet had noticed that she didn't always make it there. In spite of curfew. Some had balked at the idea of a curfew, but

2Face herself had been one of its strongest proponents. Safety of the group and all that.

Violet stopped walking. She blinked a few times and tried to remember where she was going. Lately she'd been going on autopilot a lot. *Maybe I should eat something,* she thought. *Maybe that will help.* Though she really didn't have much of an appetite. It wasn't that the limited range of food Billy/Mother produced was getting boring and not very good so much as her own lack of interest — in just about everything. Violet sighed and decided she wasn't hungry after all.

She headed on toward the dorm. When she was halfway between the girls' area and the rest rooms, she heard the shouting. Violet whirled around when she heard her name.

"Violet! Wait!" It was Olga. Tate was running close behind her.

They weren't alone. Anamull and Mo'Steel carried Tamara between them, Anamull at her shoulders. There was a dark red stain on her chest.

"Man, this is gross," Anamull muttered as they carefully lowered Tamara to the shiny floor.

Olga hovered just behind Tate. "She insisted we bring Tamara to you," Olga said. "We found her just outside the shields."

"They set her up!" Tate cried. "She wasn't wearing her body armor. They . . . they put that note in her . . . hand. . . ."

"I think it might be retribution for her bringing the Shipwright to the bridge," Olga said quietly. "The Meanies don't seem to forget. They considered it a crime against their people."

"Oh, no. Violet, can you do something, please?!"

"Get her out of here!" Violet ordered. "Now! Everybody get out."

Somebody pulled Tate out of sight. But not out of earshot. Violet looked down at the mangled and unmoving body of Sergeant Tamara Hoyle.

Violet was beginning to feel sick. She forced the bile back down her throat. She didn't want to let the — *thing* — happen. She didn't want to let the worms take over. Not again. *But I have to,* Violet told herself. *I have to try to save Tamara.*

"I'm sorry," she whispered to Tamara, and let it begin.

Violet sank deep down into herself. She concentrated on the worms, called to them, beckoned them to come out. It didn't take long for the worms to answer. Violet felt their bodies writhing in her bones. She felt them race along just under her skin, from head to neck to spine, from torso, along limbs, to feet and hands. She felt them multiplying. Hundreds becoming thousands in mere seconds. Thousands of worms invading her muscles, their pungent, loamy smell overtaking her.

It was time. Violet turned herself over to the worms, surrendered both willingly and shamefully. And then the pain began. Violet surrendered to that, too. Then her mind split apart and the pain was all — Violet was pain — and then, when she was sure, so sure she couldn't take any more, the pain began to recede, slowly but steadily.

And when the pain was gone, so was Violet. In place of a beautiful young girl was a seething, slithering mass of pea-green worms. The worms encompassed Tamara Hoyle, invaded her, bulged under her taut dark skin. And then they withdrew, shrank back into the main mass. Slowly, inevitably, the mess of worms receded and receded until . . .

Violet breathed deeply, carefully. She was herself again. And she'd done something irreversible to Tamara, but she'd also helped to give back her life.

Violet got to her knees, looked down, expected to see confusion on Tamara's face, was ready to help her sit up, ready to explain how she'd just done the impossible. But . . .

Violet stumbled back onto her heels. *No, it can't*

be! she thought wildly. No. She leaned forward and shook Tamara's arm. Nothing. The soldier's eyes remained open, blank, glassy.

"Wake up!" Violet demanded. She grabbed Tamara's shoulders and shook her. "Wake up!"

It was no good. Violet knew that now. Tamara was gone and she was going to stay that way.

So, there's a limit to this thing after all, Violet thought.

Gently, Violet removed the Meanies' note from Tamara's hand. Obviously Yago had taught one or more of his alien followers how to read and write some English. Or maybe he'd helped write the note himself — it hardly mattered anymore.

A sob rose in Violet's throat, became a wail, and she suddenly found herself crouched by Tamara's side. She had no idea how long she had been there, but she was vaguely aware of the presence of other people. She didn't protest as Anamull and Mo'Steel and D-Caf took Tamara away. When they were gone Violet's cries stopped. There was someone still there. She pushed herself to her feet.

Jobs.

"Do you . . . ?" Violet began.

"Yes," he said. "I heard about what happened."

"Oh." Violet glanced down at her feet. "So you know I couldn't help her."

"Maybe she wouldn't have wanted you to bring her back. Maybe it's better this way."

Fresh tears began to stream down Violet's face. She looked up at Jobs's face. "Maybe," she said quietly, "but I don't think so."

"Okay."

Jobs stood there, looking at her with his sad eyes. Violet could see he just didn't know what else to do.

"Maybe I should just, you know, go," he said finally.

Violet nodded. She couldn't meet his eyes anymore and turned away. But she knew Jobs was still there.

"I'm so gross, Jobs," she blurted.

"That's crazy, Violet." His tone was very serious. Even for Jobs.

"No, it's not crazy," she said, "and neither am I, okay? So just . . . I need to be by myself."

This time, Jobs walked away.

And Violet watched him go.

(CHAPTER THREE)

THIS IS WHAT MY WORLD HAS COME TO.

2Face lay on her back in the narrow bed. She couldn't sleep. Somebody was snoring. And she had a lot to think about.

2Face considered the punctures that dotted her body. They were red and puckered, like a million tiny mouths. Well, maybe not a million but at the time, when that psycho Charlie Langlow had morphed into that gruesome porcupinelike monster and impaled her, it had certainly felt like a million super-sharp arrows. That was an experience 2Face could have done without. Some of the wounds still oozed infection, and that was a major drain on her system. Even though it was over a month later, she still felt weak in the knees and woozy in the head. 2Face was pretty sure a weaker, less stubborn person would have just given up. But yeah, she definitely could have done without being made into a human pincushion.

And, 2Face thought, not for the first time, *I also could have done without Kubrick's sacrificing himself to save my life.*

Poor Kubrick. 2Face had felt a bit sorry for him, secretly, but to his face all she'd shown was strength. Strength in the face of his self-pity and his pain. She hadn't asked him to have a crush on her. Besides, she knew for sure the only reason he'd made her his target of affection was because of her messed-up face.

If only Kubrick could see me now, all full of holes, some of the wounds still oozing infection. He'd think I was really hot, 2Face thought and then immediately felt guilty for being so mean. She didn't want to feel sorry for Kubrick but she was. In a way, it was her fault he was gone and that realization didn't sit well with her.

2Face had really been thinking about things since she'd almost been killed. For the first time in a long time — more than five hundred years to be exact — 2Face found herself caring about somebody other than herself. Or her parents. Or Billy. She found herself wanting to help the other Remnants. 2Face knew she was no saint, but she wasn't completely without feelings.

So, she'd come up with a plan, a way to become useful to the others.

Tamara was gone. And she'd been their only trained warrior — her loss would hit them hard. They needed all the help they could get. Edward's chameleon act was useful, but Edward was still a little kid. Billy did what he could but his power only went so far when it came to defending them. Besides, he was really important to the basic functioning of the ship. And Mo'Steel and some of the others had basic weapons like physical strength and courage and intellect.

But it was Violet who had the real power. It was Violet — and D-Caf and Roger Dodger, who had the mutation but who they weren't sure had the power that went with it — who could bring the dead back to life, providing she got to them soon enough. And it was Violet who could give that power to 2Face.

The prospect of being infected with the wormy mutation didn't bother 2Face. Not too much, anyway. It was a small price to pay for that kind of power. Besides, she'd always been a freak to these people, hadn't she? What was one more bizarre trait?

All 2Face had to do now was convince Violet to give her the mutation. Which would mean that 2Face would have to be seriously injured. Again.

This is what my world has come to, was her last thought before she fell asleep.

Mo'Steel, his mom, and Noyze were sitting at a table in the dining area. Billy had created some human-friendly furniture when they'd retreated to the attic. Clearly the Shipwrights, the architects of the ship, hadn't expected beings from another planet to be occupying Mother, eating hamburgers and tacos.

Which is what Mo'Steel was wolfing down at the moment. He chewed heartily, eyed his mother's half-eaten taco. No matter how bad things were, Mo'Steel never lost his appetite.

"I miss Angelique — Dr. Cohen — too," Olga was saying. "We were really becoming friends."

"You can talk to me," Noyze said.

Mo'Steel felt heat rush to his face and ducked down to retie a sneaker that didn't need retying. It was weird to be in the middle of this conversation. Luckily, Noyze didn't seem to notice anything odd. When he straightened up again he saw her poking at her own half-eaten hamburger and heaving a mighty sigh.

"For me," she said, "it was like Dr. Cohen was, I don't know, not really a mother but . . ."

"Like a big sister?" Mo'Steel suggested. What

was it about this femme that got to him? He couldn't explain it even to himself. It wasn't any one thing about her. It was . . . Mo'Steel squirmed in his seat, his knee jumping double time. He didn't even know if Noyze really liked him "that way." But whatever was happening with Noyze, Mo'Steel knew he was really in trouble. And that he had a *serious* crush.

"Yeah," Noyze agreed. "Or an aunt. I mean, for a while I thought she was the only other person to survive the *Mayflower*. We thought maybe we were the only two humans alive in the entire universe."

"That's big," Mo'Steel said.

Noyze nodded, her lips pressed tightly together. "Now . . . now almost all I can think about is revenge. I want to get back at the Meanies for putting that probe in her head. I mean, we were only trying to make things right!" Noyze's voice rose and Mo'Steel flinched. "The Meanies knew us! We stayed with them! They knew we weren't going to hurt them."

"Noyze," Olga said gently, "revenge won't take away the pain. Or bring Dr. Cohen back."

"Yeah," Noyze said, bunching a napkin in her fist. "But we were wrong. We should have listened to 2Face. No negotiations."

"Don't —"

"And that Rider," Noyze said fiercely. "The one who . . ."

"I didn't think . . ." Olga began.

"I know *all* about it," Noyze said. "Roger Dodger told me. He didn't know he wasn't supposed to tell."

"I'm really sorry." Mo'Steel looked helplessly at his mother, then back to Noyze's large sad eyes. "I don't know what else to say."

Noyze looked at him then, right at him, and Mo'Steel felt like he was going to be sick.

"Thanks," Noyze whispered, and put her hand on his.

He let her take his hand in hers, wishing his mother wasn't there, hoping Noyze wouldn't mind his calloused palm. Again, Mo'Steel felt the blood rush to his face but now felt no need to hide it.

"Are you going to eat that hamburger?" he croaked.

(CHAPTER FOUR)

"I WANT NO PART OF THIS."

2Face had called a general meeting on the bridge. That way, Billy would feel most comfortable.

"Is this one of your 'tactical' meetings?" Burroway asked, his voice affecting boredom.

2Face ignored him.

"Where's Yago?" D-Caf asked.

"Where he always is, lately." Mo'Steel laughed. "Staring at a wall somewhere. You know, I had a cat who did that once. Never could tell what was going on in his head."

"Cats have a brain the size of a garbanzo bean, moron," 2Face mumbled. Yago was a lot of things, but stupid wasn't one of them. She'd bet money that Yago was secretly meeting with his Meanie followers.

"What's going on, 2Face?" Jobs asked. "Can we

start? Everyone else is here. And I don't like leaving the perimeter without a guard, even with the shields."

"I have something to tell you all," 2Face said, pitching her voice to a tone of solemnity and seriousness. "I want to have Violet's — ability."

"You what?" Olga asked.

"I want Violet to give me the ability she has. I understand that it's a mutation. It's okay. I just want to be able to help. We could use another person with the power to save lives."

D-Caf made a sound that was half snort, half yelp of horror. *Can't count on him,* 2Face thought.

"Look, I've given this a lot of thought," she said. "It's what I think is best."

Olga shook her head. "No. I can't agree to this."

Mo'Steel cleared his throat. "I'm with my mom on this," he said.

2Face turned to Jobs. He lowered his eyes, his answer clear.

2Face felt the frustration mount. She hadn't expected everyone to be enthusiastic about her plan but she also hadn't expected such total resistance.

She turned to Tate. The girl looked incredibly

tired. Since Tamara's death her eyes seemed devoid of life. 2Face wished she'd get over it.

"I want no part of this," Tate said, her voice husky with unshed tears.

"I'll take that as a 'yes,'" 2Face said defiantly. "Noyze?"

"I . . ." Noyze looked right at 2Face, the momentary look of confusion on her face clearing. "I'm sorry. Count me out, too."

Olga whispered, "Good girl."

"I think it's cool," Edward said suddenly. "Then we can be superheroes together."

2Face felt a pang of conscience. Edward shouldn't be involved in this decision. He was only a kid. He wasn't thinking straight. Still, it was the first positive vote. She'd take it.

"Thanks, kid," she said, smiling.

"Roger Dodger got the worms but he hasn't tried to save anyone so we don't know if he got the power," Anamull pointed out. "What if you don't get it?"

2Face stood firm. "I'll take my chances."

"Whatever." Anamull shrugged. "I think you're a nut, but do what you want to do."

This was more like it. Two votes. 2Face knew she could force the issue but didn't want it to be that way. She wanted their support. She wanted to come out clean.

"Burroway?" she said. He just might be intimidated into seeing her point of view.

Burroway shot a glance at Olga, then at Violet. *He doesn't even have a mind of his own,* 2Face thought, barely suppressing a sneer of contempt.

"I think it's a disgusting idea," he said, his voice full of false bravado.

"Big surprise," 2Face muttered.

"I want to know what Billy thinks," she said. 2Face walked over to where Billy stood by a bank of small view screens. His hands hung at his sides and his face seemed paler than ever. Behind her, 2Face heard the low sounds of protest.

2Face took Billy's hand in hers. "You're my friend," she whispered. "Tell me what you think."

For a moment Billy was silent. Then he spoke.

"I . . . I came so close to losing you once before," he said, looking at 2Face and no one else. "I don't know if I could stand really losing you for good."

2Face could tell that it was taking every ounce of Billy's strength to talk so personally in front of all these people. She was proud of him for it.

"But you won't lose me, Billy," 2Face said. "Because I'll come right back."

Billy shook his head. His thick black hair looked shaggy, 2Face noted. "But what if Violet can't, for some reason, bring you back? What then? We don't know for sure why she couldn't help Tamara."

"That's what I said," Anamull called out. "We don't know nothin'."

2Face looked over her shoulder at him and frowned. When she turned back to face Billy, the frown was gone. "Billy, look, nothing is guaranteed in life. Especially not here. You know that."

"I know," Billy said, almost angry now. "I know there's nothing I can do about the people who are gone. But there is something I can do about your wanting to get hurt to get this ability. I can ask you not to do it. No, I can *tell* you not to do it. Maybe you won't listen to me but I can tell you how I feel."

The silence following Billy's words was heavy. Heavy with relief. 2Face pulled her hand from Billy's and rejoined the group. This was not going at all well.

"Look," 2Face said irritably, feeling betrayed, "it really only matters what Violet thinks. Or D-Caf. Or Roger Dodger."

"Leave them out of it!" Violet snapped. D-Caf took a step farther away from the group. 2Face saw Roger Dodger step behind Tate.

"Okay. Fine. But Violet, you see the value here, don't you? So?" 2Face pressed.

Violet's expression hardened into something intractable and for a split second 2Face actually felt afraid of her.

"Absolutely not," Violet said.

(CHAPTER FIVE)

IT HADN'T FELT THE WAY SHE'D THOUGHT IT WOULD FEEL.

Month Four

Yago looked out through the shield at the dismal, watery environment that was the Riders' home. He was on guard duty and was bored. Nothing had happened in the past hour; he'd seen not one Rider or anti-Yago Meanie, the ones who called themselves the True Children of Mother. Enemy attacks had been fewer and farther between the closer the ship came to Earth, and Yago couldn't figure out why. You couldn't call the situation a truce or stalemate.

Uneasy. Something was up; either the Meanies were afraid of something or they were planning a huge sneak attack. Automatically, Yago felt for his fléchette gun and realized it wasn't there in his belt. It wasn't fair. Yago wasn't allowed to carry a weapon when on duty because 2Face had told him they didn't trust him not to do something stupid.

Yago had to work off some of the energy building inside so he began to pace the length of his station, every so often giving a desultory glance out into the coppery marsh. Talk about doing something stupid! Of course he'd heard what 2Face had tried to get Violet to do for her and it made him mad. Who did that freak think she was, muscling in on what, by right, was his? Yago knew 2Face's offer was all about 2Face — and about her alliance with Billy. She was trying to consolidate power, locate it all in herself and the little weirdo.

Well, Yago was no saint courting martyrdom. He was through trying to bring the Remnants to the light of his way. He'd tried to save the Remnants by calling in his own Meanie force, even though they were severely outnumbered by the unenlightened Children. But had anyone thanked him for his efforts? No. True, Yago admitted serenely, his motives had been less than altruistic, but what did that matter? The point remained that he had offered the services of his own Meanies, had seen them brutally cut down, and had received in return not one shred of thanks, not one iota of appreciation.

Yago finally stopped his pacing, squinted hard out through the shields. Nothing. All was eerily still, except for the extremely bendy trees native to Mother's default environment. Three more hours to go.

Fine, Yago thought, *let 2Face do what deluded things she'd do. Let them all follow her like frightened sheep.* It wouldn't matter one way or the other to Yago. Because he was going to find a way out.

D-Caf poked at the cupcake on the table in front of him. It was supposed to be a Hostess cupcake, the kind with the chocolate icing and white squiggle on top and cream in the middle. His brother had told him once that the cream was just grease, but D-Caf hadn't cared. He liked the taste. Mark had laughed and said, "You'd eat anything, wouldn't you?"

That wasn't true, that he'd eat anything. But the memory had made him lose interest in the cupcake and he sighed.

D-Caf was alone in the dining area. That wasn't great. Ever since he'd been brought back by Violet he'd tried to avoid being alone too much. Being alone meant remembering the dream he'd had while he was "gone."

This dream or vision bothered him. He wished he could figure it out.

D-Caf's head shot up when someone came into the room. It was Roger Dodger.

"Hey," D-Caf said.

"Hey," Roger Dodger said back.

"Uh, you want this cupcake?"

Roger Dodger shrugged. "Okay. Thanks." He sat down across from D-Caf, reached for the cupcake, and began to peel away the paper.

"Kinda stupid how Billy makes them with the paper, right?" D-Caf said with a nervous laugh.

"I guess."

D-Caf waited while the kid stuffed the entire cupcake into his mouth, chewed messily, then swallowed.

"My dad taught me how to do that," Roger Dodger said finally. "My mom hated it."

"Look," D-Caf said, "I have a question about what happened to you."

Roger Dodger gave him a look that D-Caf thought might mean, "You're freaky." But he pressed on.

"Do you ever think about it, the time you were actually dead? Before Violet —"

"Yeah," the kid said quickly. "I saw something."

"Like a dream?" D-Caf felt his face getting warm with excitement.

Roger Dodger nodded. "I never told anyone about it."

"Me, too," D-Caf said. "I saw something and I never told anyone about it. I figured they wouldn't understand."

D-Caf watched Roger Dodger closely. The kid chewed his lip and looked away from him.

"You wanna hear what I saw?" D-Caf said. "And you can tell me what you saw."

"Okay." Roger Dodger looked back at D-Caf. He looked scared. "But let's swear not to tell anyone else."

D-Caf grinned thankfully. "Deal. Want another cupcake?"

CHAPTER SIX

"HOW COULD YOU DO THIS?!"

2Face made her way to the west perimeter guard station. Before she left she'd checked the posted schedule of duty. And she knew Violet would be there. 2Face didn't know if Violet would be alone. It was now or never.

The guard station came into view; beyond the shields 2Face could see the coppery swamp. Violet wasn't alone. Mo'Steel was with her.

2Face walked quietly toward them. She wanted the advantage of surprise. When she was no more than two yards behind Violet and Mo'Steel, she cleared her throat. And threw out the Rider boomerang she'd taken from Violet's basement after Roger Dodger's accident. She had no intention of catching it when it returned to her.

* * *

"How could yo do this?!" Violet's voice was flat with anger. She stood over 2Face's body and began to call the worms. She gave 2Face the mutation. When it was done, 2Face opened her eyes.

Without another word, Violet walked away. And didn't look back.

It hadn't felt the way she'd thought it would feel. In fact, 2Face realized, it hadn't felt like anything at all. One second she was throwing the boomerang. The next — nothing. Then she was *there* again, and Violet was walking away and Mo'Steel . . .

2Face turned her head to see if he was still around and winced. Ow. Ow-ow-ow. She was achy all over, like when she'd had the flu, just one big miserable ache.

Carefully, 2Face got to her feet. The weapon was still there on the ground. 2Face picked it up, stuck it in the waistband of her pants. *Well,* she thought, *I've made more enemies. But it's going to be worth it in the long run.* She headed for the elevator, which would take her to the dining area. Forcing Violet to give her the mutation had been hungry work; she'd need to eat, buck up her strength, before going on guard duty later. As the elevator made its way to the attic she wondered about her new power. She wondered if it worked on beings other than humans. Or if it only worked on sentient beings. 2Face was eager to explore the limits and possibilities of the mutation. And she had a feeling there'd be plenty of opportunities ahead.

Mo'Steel found his friend in the lab. Jobs was in the middle of a calculation concerning — something — but Mo'Steel needed to talk to him. About 2Face.

"I always thought she was a little off, but . . . I don't know, Duck. I never saw anyone do something so — super wacko!"

Jobs just nodded.

2Face had wanted the mutation. And she did what she had to do to get it. Mo'Steel just couldn't get his mind around that.

"So, now she's like Violet and D-Caf and Roger Dodger, sort of," Mo'Steel said. "And Yago's got that magic touch thing and Edward . . . You think anyone else has something going on, something they're not — let's say — sharing?"

"I don't know," Jobs admitted. "It's very possible."

Mo'Steel twitched with nervous energy. "Because it's possible, 'migo, possible that someone's got some mutation or redesign, whatever, that could make him — or her — turn against the rest of us. Right?"

Jobs laughed a little, then smiled at his friend. "Since when did you become paranoid?"

"You never considered it?" Mo'Steel was dead serious.

"Yeah," Jobs said, "of course." He put down the pencil he'd been twirling. "I just don't want to get too suspicious. I don't want everyone looking over their shoulder, afraid. There are so few of us left. We've got to try to deal with all this kind of stuff before we really start to turn on one another."

"And the Troika," Mo'Steel pointed out. "Call me crazy, but I don't think they want to be buddies. And they're the ones who are the most out there. The most evolved, whatever you want to call it."

"We don't know for sure about Duncan," Jobs said reasonably.

"Yeah, we do. Come on, if he's Amelia's buddy, and Charlie's, he's got something freaky inside. *No doubt.*" Mo'Steel considered. "Jobs? You think Violet and them are more like the Troika now than like us?"

Jobs sighed. "I have no idea, Mo."

There was something else on Mo'Steel's mind. "There are still people missing from the *Mayflower,*" Mo'Steel said. "Amelia said, what, that they hadn't been able to make the transition or something? That they weren't like her and Charlie and Duncan. You ever wonder where they are?"

"I think it's a pretty good guess that they didn't make it," Jobs said.

The look on Mo'Steel's face said it was not the answer he expected to hear.

(CHAPTER SEVEN)

I NEED TO DO THIS.

Month Five

"Ready, 'migo?"

"As I'll ever be."

Jobs and Mo'Steel stood at the mouth of the tube, one of many such dark, narrow holes throughout the ship. Long ago they'd discovered that these tubes were part of the original architecture of the ship. And while no one was certain of their original purpose, it was clear they were intended for some form of extravehicular activity, maybe maintenance to the outside of the ship, maybe just for fun. If the Shipwrights were into that sort of thing. Somehow, Jobs doubted it.

Riding the tubes wasn't an experience Jobs particularly enjoyed. But he had to do it now, when Mother was, according to Billy's calculations, approximately one month, thirty days, away from what was left of Earth. Jobs wanted to get a closer look at the planet — their old home. The place they might call home again. He wanted to get whatever information he could in order to help prepare them for whatever they might encounter when they finally got there.

But most of all, Jobs wanted to see Earth. He'd loved his home. He still did. Sometimes in Billy's created "night," as he was struggling to fall asleep, he thought of home. Of his parents and friends and people he would never see again. He thought of school and his old room and other random memories.

Jobs wanted to go home.

Jobs knew he could have asked Mo'Steel to ride the tubes in his place. Or at least go with him. In most things, he trusted Mo'Steel more than he trusted himself. But Jobs felt a weird kind of ownership when it came to what was left of Earth. He'd discovered it, or rediscovered it. He'd urged the Remnants to go home. Now he wanted to be the first to see it up close.

"You don't come back in fifteen," Mo'Steel said, "I'm coming to get you, Duck."

Jobs grinned. "I'm holding you to that."

Jobs took a deep breath, tried to calm his tingling nerves. *Just jump,* he told himself. So he did, and then began the big drop, the falling and tumbling, the shooting-past flashes of dark red shapes and spooky forms. Even though he'd done it all before the panic still flooded his brain. And then the worst part of the "ride." Jobs felt like he was suffocating, knew he wasn't, and tried to calm himself. He passed through the warm, taffylike substance, let it coat him from head to toe. Soon Jobs was encased in the goo space suit, covered with the sticky, pliable stuff that would allow him to move freely just outside the ship, that would keep him safe from radiation and the fire of passing meteors and the deadly cold of space and the blinding brightness of the sun — and any other miscellaneous hazards the universe might throw his way.

Jobs couldn't hear anything because there were no air molecules to knock around and create sound. Even if there was sound, what would there be to hear but the roar of Mother's engines? He could see and that was what mattered.

With some awkwardness, Jobs oriented himself so that he was facing the mass that was Earth and its moon, now just one big mashed-together lump.

Jobs blinked, shut his eyes hard, and then opened them wide. No. It wasn't a mistake. But it sure wasn't what he'd expected to see. And it wasn't what he'd seen on his first virtual-reality excursions. It wasn't what he'd shown Mo'Steel. What he saw now made no sense. *Wait.* Jobs corrected his own panicked thinking. *It makes sense. I just have to find out why.*

From what he could see, it . . . it was a place of extremes.

One huge side — a half? More than half? — of the larger piece, what was left of the earth, was in complete darkness. Jobs guessed that it was probably very cold. It was a wasteland.

The other side was facing the sun. It was bright beyond tolerance and bombarded by intense radiation. Probably uninhabitable as well, the terrain sharp with needlelike protrusions.

Yin and yang, Jobs thought. One part exists because of the other. Equal and opposite. Good and bad, though in this case, which part was good and which bad? No shades of gray.

Except that between these two impossible environments there seemed to be a strip of land, not very wide, maybe a couple of hundred miles across — maybe more — that seemed to exist in a kind of dry mist. It was a shadow world, the land jagged and mountainous in places, at others oddly flat.

Where is the water? Jobs thought. *Where are the trees?* There was nothing to see. And suddenly he realized just how badly he'd wanted to see a planet teeming with life. Earth. His home.

He wanted to see oceans and rivers, lakes and streams. He wanted to see trees and grasses, animals — and humans. But there was nothing, not even a glimmer of artificial light, no more big cities burning bright. *Nothing.*

Jobs began to make educated guesses about the atmosphere and gravity of this compartmentalized planet. Thin atmosphere, low gravity. Life on the surface, if it could exist at all, could exist only in the Shadow Zone. Provided its air wasn't still toxic. Provided its soil was more than just ash and dead matter. Provided there was water. There was no possibility of life without water. Not even bacteria could live without it.

Okay, he thought. *Figure this out.* Water. Oceans. There could be vast expanses of frozen seas in the Dark Zone. It was possible. And they might be accessible after all, chunks of ice could be brought back to the Shadow Zone where they would be thawed and purified for use as drinking water. Thawed for use as energy.

Maybe.

And it was possible there were vast expanses of bubbling, boiling seas on the Bright Zone. Fiery seas that could for some unexpected or unknown reason surge up and spill over into the Shadow Zone. . . . *We'd be trapped between two deadly extremes,* Jobs thought morbidly. *Fire and ice.*

Jobs began to focus on the smaller chunk of the planet. The part that had once been Earth's moon. Thin atmosphere, no visible bodies of water. Gray and pockmarked with craters of varying shapes and sizes. Uninhabitable. No doubt about that.

What else had he seen back then, going VR? Jobs propelled himself to the right, then left in the weirdly easy way the goo suit allowed him to move. He still couldn't spot Mars. Jobs recognized other planets of Earth's solar system. There was Jupiter, still seeming far too bright to be the Jupiter he'd studied back in school. There was Earth's sun, right where it should be. But pre-Rock facts weren't necessarily post-Rock facts, were they?

Jobs made a decision. He knew he shouldn't stay outside the ship much longer. There were some restrictions to the goo suit. But all Jobs could think about was Earth. He felt he *had* to stay and watch. He had to wait and observe. Maybe he'd missed something. Maybe his mind was playing tricks on him. Maybe if he hung on as long as he could something — what? — would happen. Something good.

I hope Mo'Steel doesn't come riding to the rescue, Jobs thought. *I need to do this.*

Jobs waited. Time passed, how much he didn't know. At some point he noticed he was having trouble breathing. At some point after that he felt slightly light-headed and saw with vague alarm that his goo suit was slowly beginning to dissolve.

I should go in now, he thought fuzzily, but stayed where he was.

Jobs waited long enough to recognize yet another dismal fact. Earth no longer rotated. It had its orbit, but Earth, with its attached moon, no longer rotated. The Dark Zone remained dark and the Bright Zone remained bright.

Jobs felt like he was going to be sick. Right there in his goo suit — *it looks thinner, doesn't it?* he thought, staring at his hand.

Jobs fought down the bile, and took as deep a breath as he could, steadied himself, figured he'd just cut minutes off what air remained. He turned awkwardly away from the dismal sight, and Mother filled his field of vision. A vast topography of unexplained structures, glimmering lights, and metal plates. An immense machine.

Jobs had never felt so alone. Who could he talk to about what he'd seen? Could he tell Mo'Steel his doubts? Violet? No. It was because of him, Jobs, that they'd chosen to break the Big Compromise and head for Earth. Because of what he'd told everyone he'd seen, planet Earth, not fully destroyed, still in orbit, seeming to have a few bodies of water, smaller sections of green.

He'd made a mistake. A huge one.

But even as he contemplated this through an increasingly fuzzy head he knew what he had to do. He'd go back. And he'd tell them the truth.

Without a final glimpse of Earth, Jobs propelled himself up toward the ship. It was tough going. The goo suit seemed to have molded so closely to his skin it was like the skin itself. Thin. Vulnerable.

The exterior mouth of the tube opened for him. With every last ounce of energy Jobs climbed upward through space, got into the tube, lost the remains of the goo suit, emerged, stumbling, gasping, from the interior mouth of the tube.

"S'up, Duck?"

Jobs regained his balance, said, "What?"

"You're back just in time," Mo'Steel said grimly. "Thought I was gonna have to take a little ride."

(CHAPTER EIGHT)

WHAT WOULD HAPPEN WOULD HAPPEN.

Month Six

They were gathered on the bridge. No one had suggested they all get together but they had, one by one, 2Face first, Yago last. Violet wondered if someone should be on perimeter guard duty and then shrugged off the thought. It didn't seem to matter any longer. "Prepare for landing," Violet whispered to herself.

Though she'd been on the bridge innumerable times, the massive open space still awed her. There were dozens of computer-interface chairs, designed for Shipwrights, constructed by Shipwrights. They'd used the chairs to interface with Mother. Billy, who'd incorporated Mother — literally — didn't need an interface chair to communicate with her. In some weird way, Billy was Mother and Mother was Billy. It gave Violet a headache when she thought about it too much.

Violet turned her attention from the bridge to her companions. The tension was palpable. Violet could feel it in her bones, her own excitement and dread compounded by the volatile, mixed-up feelings of the others.

When Jobs first told Violet about his find, she hadn't wanted to take the ship back to Earth. The prospect had seemed too horribly sad, doomed. "You can't go home again," she'd said, and she'd believed that. Then she'd been attacked by Yago's faction of Meanies and Violet had changed her mind. Or had she? She'd been so angry she'd just joined up with 2Face and supported their breaking the Big Compromise.

But, Violet thought as she watched their approach to a badly damaged Earth, *I still believe there is no such thing as going home.*

Next time — if there was a next time — she'd keep her mouth shut.

Noyze wished Dr. Cohen were around to experience all of this. Not that Noyze was exactly alone without her friend. There was Mo'Steel, for one, and his mom. Still, Noyze felt lonely watching Earth get closer and closer, knowing she was zooming closer and closer to it. This was way scarier than just before she was put under on the *Mayflower*. This was way, way scarier.

She knew she should probably feel like she was going home but she didn't. She just felt like she was being dropped helplessly into a very scary future.

Mo'Steel took her hand. Noyze held on tight.

Mo'Steel was nothing if not calm. It was too late to turn back now, wasn't it? The direction had been set and they would just keep moving ahead, like anybody set in motion, like when you locked your boots on your skis and pushed off and started the twenty-, thirty-mile-an-hour *whoosh* down the mountain. He and the other Remnants would just keep rolling on until something got in their way and they couldn't roll any farther.

It was okay. It would have to be.

Mo'Steel snuck a glance at Noyze. He couldn't believe he'd had the nerve to hold her hand but he had. But maybe it hadn't been about nerve. Mo'Steel thought and realized it had been more like an instinct. One second his hand was beating a rhythm on his thigh; the next, it was wrapped around Noyze's hand. Easy as that.

And if anyone teased him about it he'd . . .

Mo'Steel gave Noyze's hand a quick squeeze. Well, he'd probably just grin.

Daniel Burroway felt downright positive for the first time since they'd awakened on board that rickety old tin can, the *Mayflower*.

Once on Earth he would become the patriarch of a brave new world. The younger boys were no threat to him. He knew they didn't like him and easily attributed that to their jealousy of an older, accomplished man. They were merely untried adolescents, eager for notice, making fools of themselves in the process.

Burroway grimaced as he watched Anamull sneak up behind D-Caf and give him a wedgie.

Things will be different once we reach Earth, he thought. *My time will come.*

Olga had never felt so overwhelmed. Never so frightened, never so desperately sure she wouldn't be able to handle what her life would become. And, at the same time, so absolutely excited and eager and, yes, triumphant! She was going home.

Olga was ready.

*   *   *

Tate stood off by herself, hands shoved deep into the front pockets of her baggy jeans. She didn't belong here with the others, she thought. She felt — alone, isolated. She tried to be excited about the fact that the ship was soon going to land on Earth. She tried to be interested in the — remote — possibility that soon she might come face-to-face with the descendants of human beings who had actually survived the Rock all those years ago. Tate tried to be afraid and nervous, brave and courageous. She tried to care one way or the other. But she couldn't feel anything.

Tate turned away from the view of Earth.

"They are fools," Amelia said.

"Idiots," Charlie Langlow added.

Duncan Choate grinned. "Hey, I kind of like them."

CHAPTER NINE

HOMEWARD BOUND.

Anamull was excited. He was scared, too, but he wasn't going to let anyone know that. What, so someone could pat him on the head or something? Feel sorry for him? No way. He was doing a good job of hiding his fear by annoying D-Caf and Roger Dodger, playing the bully.

Anamull had had a lot of adventures since boarding the *Mayflower* more than five hundred years ago. Way more than he'd have had if the Rock hadn't decided to crash into Earth and everything had gone on like normal.

Anamull was pretty happy about that. Most of the time.

ADD. That's what his teachers and doctors and parents had told him he "suffered from." Please. Like Attention Deficit Disorder made you sick or something. They'd made him take some medicine that was supposed to calm him down or something. Anamull laughed out loud at the memory. D-Caf jumped, looked at him. Anamull sneered and the twitch turned away.

Anamull moved closer to the medium-sized screen that showed planet Earth and grinned.

D-Caf watched space through the giant ceiling screen. It was pretty, so black, with distant stars twinkling bravely. Watching space helped settle D-Caf's nerves. He was concerned about going back to Earth. Concerned and excited. He hoped that once they were back on Earth he'd have a chance to further redeem himself in the eyes of the others. He'd already come a long way. He'd turned from Yago and the others had accepted him, if not enthusiastically then without complaint. And now he might just have the same power Violet did; he might be able to bring a person back to life. That possibility helped make him okay in the eyes of the others — didn't it?

D-Caf lowered his gaze and turned to the view screen showing home.

Roger Dodger was tired of standing around so he flopped into one of the disconnected, oversized computer-interface chairs the Shipwrights had left behind. It was okay. Billy had said nothing bad would happen to him if he sat there.

He heard something and looked to the right. He barely made out Edward against the wall and smiled. A piece of the wall seemed to tremble. They all had something. He could go wormy. Edward could just blend in and nearly disappear.

Roger Dodger was glad he wasn't going home alone.

Edward knew he was hardly visible. He knew that if anyone in the room looked at him they wouldn't see him but a patch of dull smooth metal wall.

He wasn't trying to blend in. Sometimes he did try but most times he didn't have to do anything at all. He just blended in. He just went all chameleon.

When Edward had left Earth he'd been just an average, kind of quiet kid, overshadowed by his brilliant big brother. He hadn't minded. But now he was going back to Earth and he was very, very different. Jobs had told him it was pretty sure nobody had survived the Rock. And even if they had they'd be gone now because a lot of time had passed since then. Still, Edward wished he'd find some of his friends on Earth. He really, really wished he could show Todd and Jason what he could do! They had been in his class back home. They'd be so jealous! Now you see me, now you don't.

That was really all Edward hoped to find back on Earth. For now, he'd just play he was the wall and wave to Roger Dodger, who'd spotted him.

Jobs kept his eyes glued to the view screen set on Earth. His right foot tapped the floor; his left hand picked at the cuticles of his right hand.

Since Jobs had come back from his "trip" outside Mother, when he'd seen the devastated planet, when he'd spent the first hour back on board getting sick and enduring the worse headache ever — a migraine, Olga told him, shooting, viselike pain, flashing lights behind his eyelids — since he'd come back he'd felt like a tightly wound spring, ready to *POP!*

It was like a role reversal, Jobs being the keyed-up one, Mo'Steel being the opposite. At first, when Mo'Steel had asked what Jobs had seen, he'd said, "Nothing much," which wasn't exactly a lie. But Mo'Steel had taken one look at the shreds of Jobs's goo suit and at his friend's green face, raised an eyebrow, and said, "Spill it, 'migo." So he had, when he had recovered enough. Mo'Steel had been a bit down ever since. Nothing the others would notice, but Jobs knew Mo'Steel too well not to see his friend was really troubled by the news.

Billy hadn't asked for a report at all. But, Jobs had given him one. 2Face had been there, too. Billy had been quiet, his face impassive. 2Face had flushed — with anger or fear, Jobs couldn't tell. Her voice grim, she'd told them she'd break the news to the others and she had. Jobs hadn't had the heart — or the nerve — to stop her.

Bottom line: He'd been afraid of what the others would do to him — what the others would think of him — when they learned they were headed for a seemingly dead planet.

Amazingly, the others had taken the news well. As well as could be expected. It occurred to Jobs that by now, none of them had much more than a shred of hope inside — if that much. No one had much expectation of anything but more grim death.

Still, Jobs wished they'd stuck to an earlier plan. After his excursion he'd suggested they not actually land the ship but keep it in orbit as close above Earth as was necessary. They'd find a way to send two or three people down to check it out, try to get a reading on the oxygen situation, and see if it was worth bringing everybody down.

Jobs had been surprised when they shot his idea

down. Seemed now that they were so close, everyone just wanted to "do it," get it over with.

So that's what they were doing. Every one of them was on the bridge with Billy, keeping track of the action as he brought the ship down through Earth's atmosphere — whatever was left of it.

Jobs turned away from the view screen and began to walk around the bridge. For the past few days he had been thinking about a book he'd read when he was about ten. He'd found it on his father's bookshelf. The book was called *Stranger in a Strange Land* and it was by a guy named Heinlein. Jobs had enjoyed it, though at the time some of the story was too grown up for him. Basically, it was about a guy who'd been born on Mars to scientist parents who died. The guy had been raised by Martians, had become a Martian in most ways. Years later another expedition from Earth found him and brought him back to Earth. The guy was the stranger of the title. The strange land was Earth.

Jobs stopped pacing and sighed. He felt very much like the main character in that book, about to be dropped into a place supposed to be his home. A place he remembered all too well. But these days a place he knew absolutely nothing about.

Stranger in a strange land.

* * *

Billy was concentrating, connecting with Mother, bringing her down. Jobs had told him to land in an area he'd charted out, an area Jobs called the Shadow Zone. That was fine by Billy.

Billy had gone along with what 2Face and some of the others had wanted. He'd taken Mother off the course set by the Shipwrights long, long ago. He'd taken her to Earth. And while they were on Earth he'd continue to keep Mother safe from interference by the Meanies, the Riders, the Troika.

The Troika frightened Billy. Because they were unknowable to him. And he couldn't figure out *why* they were unknowable. He wanted to know about the Troika and their connection — his own connection — to the Ancient Enemy, as well as to the human race. Billy had plenty of work cut out for him aside from exploring the remains of planet Earth.

And he wouldn't abandon Mother. He wasn't quite sure what abandonment would entail, but he did know he wouldn't leave the ship itself. He didn't think anyone would object. Let the others explore. He'd stay here.

Billy looked over at 2Face and wondered what she was thinking. He used to think he knew her, a little anyway. But after she'd forced Violet to give her the mutation, he knew he didn't really know her. At all. And he didn't want to.

2Face sensed Billy watching her, turned to him and smiled. He smiled back wanly.

Her smile had been forced. The reality was that 2Face felt anything but happy. What she felt was the pressure of authorship. To a large extent she'd orchestrated this moment, inspired it, too. If this was a bust, if Earth turned out to be the dead planet Jobs now thought it was, people were going to blame her. Though all she'd done was step up for their rights against the tyranny of the Meanies. Still, the thought of failure loomed large in 2Face's mind and threatened her. She took a deep breath.

She could do this. All she had to do now was keep her eyes wide open and her brain on alert.

2Face looked again at Billy, his eyes shut, communing with Mother.

"Bring it on," she said to the universe.

Yago stood off by himself. He wasn't even sure what he was doing up on the bridge. He hadn't been part of the decision to turn Mother around, to alter her course drastically, to return to planet Earth. He didn't want anything to do with Earth. His future lay elsewhere.

Yago came to a decision, one that had been forming for the past few months. Quietly, he slipped from the bridge. There was much still to be done.

"Touchdown," Jobs breathed. "Thanks, Billy."

And then the cheering began.

"They're going to regret this." Amelia turned to her comrades. "*All* of them."

CHAPTER TEN

"THERE'S, LIKE, NOTHING HERE."

The cheering had stopped. The mood of anticipation had been replaced by quiet introspection. Jobs had unthinkingly repressed his excitement and it seemed the others had, too. Jobs knew the excitement was still there, underneath, but suddenly it was tempered by the reality of NOW. Now it was time to walk on Earth.

There'd been no Meanie or Rider or Troika attacks during the landing process. Jobs found that interesting, as it had been a time of vulnerability for the Remnants. It made him wonder what their shipboard enemies were planning. Because they had to be planning something, some attack or maybe even a conciliatory approach, though that seemed unlikely. Amelia, at least, was not the sort to just fade away.

Well, Jobs thought, *we aren't going to sit around and wait for something bad to happen.* There was work to do. They would explore a little bit of the planet. They wouldn't go far, just stick around the base of the ship.

Jobs insisted they divide into two groups. The first was composed of Jobs, Violet, Yago, D-Caf, Anamull, Edward, and 2Face. Mo'Steel, Olga, Burroway, Roger Dodger, Tate, and Noyze were in the second group.

Billy was staying on the ship. Olga and Violet had exchanged glances when he'd made this announcement. Jobs had gotten the feeling something about Billy's staying on board worried them. Jobs had a few issues with Billy's decision, too. But he kept his mouth shut.

Everyone made sure that they were equipped with basic rations — a half liter of water each and some crackers. They also carried lead-lined bags and wore special gloves Jobs and Billy created for bringing anything interesting back to the ship. Each person had a small oxygen tank, a flashlight, and some rope. On a bandolier Jobs, Mo'Steel, Anamull, Violet, Tate, and D-Caf each sported a weapon either from the Meanies, the Riders, or produced by Billy/Mother: A boomerang. A mini-missile. A specially altered handheld fléchette gun. A crossbow. A pistol.

"Everybody ready for this?" Jobs called to the

first group. The second group were still on the bridge with Billy.

"Yeah. We're ready," 2Face replied.

A panel in one of the gray-green walls shimmered and disappeared and an oddly narrow ramp was lowered. Mo'Steel called it a "Billy-ramp" because the Shipwrights obviously had had no use for certain types of landing gear, but Billy knew that Jobs and the others would need a way off — or back on board — the ship.

No toxic fumes rushed in. No one rushed to put on their oxygen masks. As if by unspoken agreement, the group began to move slowly down the ramp.

Jobs's mouth felt as if he'd just swallowed a handful of sand. This was it.

Once they'd stepped off the ramp and onto Earth's surface Jobs began to breathe again. He'd been so nervous he wasn't even aware that he'd been holding his breath. The air was filled with dust, and it billowed gently at their feet with each uncertain step. Job didn't feel hot or cold. He didn't really feel anything. He was aware of his lungs working harder in the thin atmosphere but he was in no pain.

"We're probably going to need a little more oxygen," he said to the others, "but otherwise it looks like this is doable." Jobs felt tears begin to sting his eyes but he blinked them away. "There doesn't seem to be as much gravity as we're used to, but we're not going to float off into space."

"Not floating away is a good thing," Violet murmured.

"Whoa. Mother sure is one butt-ugly ship!" Anamull said. He stared wide-eyed at the vehicle. "I mean, I never saw it from the outside."

"It probably — looks much cooler in space," D-Caf said seriously, breathing heavily. "But you're right. Down here — it's just some — big old blob or something."

Jobs looked back at Anamull and D-Caf and wondered if they cared at all about being back on Earth. They didn't seem to notice one way or the other.

Jobs certainly cared about being back. He surveyed what could be seen. And from where he stood at the foot of the ship's ramp both the Dark and the Bright Zones were in the distance. Jobs guessed that if they were to walk, it would probably take them almost twenty-four hours to reach either zone. If they should ever have to actually go there. Jobs was hoping it was a big if.

"Let's concentrate on Earth," Jobs said quickly.

"It's . . . beautiful," Violet said. She took a few

rapid breaths, then went on. "In a terribly depressing sort of way."

Jobs silently agreed with Violet, and turned to his left and then to his right. He glanced up at the sky. There wasn't even a cloud in the sky to break the monotony of the uniform gray that surrounded them. And oddly enough, there wasn't a visible horizon.

"I think it's pretty boring." Anamull gestured at the expanse of waste. "There's, like, nothing here. Now what?"

"You need to back off!" Jobs snapped.

"Hey! No one's attacking you, dude," Anamull retorted. "Lighten up."

D-Caf's chest visibly rose and fell. His speech was slow and frequently broken up by his involuntary attempts to suck more oxygen out of the air. "I thought . . . there'd be . . . water. A . . . lake, something."

"There might be," 2Face said. "We just don't know yet."

Yago was silent. "You all right?" Jobs asked him. Yago nodded, looked skyward. Jobs noted that Yago's expression was blank, unreadable, even more empty than his usual blissed-out expression.

Jobs shook his head, turned, watched as Edward

blended, became part of the all-over gray landscape, ash and dust.

Jobs flashed on the seven billion dead; on all the cities that were decimated; on the rich, millennia-old cultures lost. His mind was flooded with images of the small, simple things that had made life so amazing. Pizza with extra cheese and rock and roll and hanging out with Mo after school and raindrops on dark green leaves and girls like Cordelia.

He thought of all these things and more in the face of the dustbowl before him. And the sadness made him stumble.

Mo'Steel looked out at the gray expanse. The first group had gone out and come back without any real problems. But they hadn't found any signs of life. So far, neither had Mo'Steel's group.

He let himself bounce in place for a while, pushing off first with both feet, then one, then the other, then both again. There had to be some benefit to this place. If relatively low gravity was all there was, he'd take it. And he was in pretty good shape — so he was having very minor trouble breathing while, well, bouncing.

The others weren't so lucky. Burroway's breathing was labored. Mo'Steel's mom wasn't doing so bad in the breathing department, but said she felt a headache coming on. Noyze confessed to feeling nauseous; Mo'Steel encouraged her to suck up her spare oxygen and then use his. Tate and Roger Dodger seemed at about the same level of discomfort — mild.

"I would love to see a flower," Olga said suddenly, rubbing her temples. "A peony maybe, all lush and pink."

"A dolphin jumping over the waves." That was Noyze. "The water all sparkling with sunlight."

Tate smiled. "The sound of leaves rustling in the fall." Took a breath. "The smell of an autumn bonfire."

"A club," Mo'Steel said.

Burroway laughed derisively, finished with a choke. "What?"

"A club. A dance club. Lots of people having fun. Music. Strobes. Energy. That's what I'm missing most. People."

"What do you miss most, Mr. Burroway?" Roger Dodger asked.

The question seemed to startle him. He frowned.

"I . . . I don't know. I . . . I guess I haven't really thought about it."

The answer seemed to disappoint Roger Dodger. Mo'Steel slung an arm around the kid's shoulder. "I'm sure Mr. Burroway misses his family most, kid. Isn't that right, Mr. Burroway?"

Burroway glared at Mo'Steel, then colored. "Yes, that's right. I miss my family, of course." Labored breathing. "My wife and children."

Mo'Steel gave Roger Dodger a one-armed hug and said, "Just like you miss your family, huh, 'migo?"

"Yeah," Roger Dodger answered eagerly. "Them and my dog and snowstorms. I had a cool sled and I'd build snowmen and stuff. My dog, his name was Bozo, he liked to play in the snow, too. I miss that."

"Maybe somed —" Mo'Steel caught himself, smiled awkwardly. No point in raising the kid's hopes. Didn't look like it was going to snow anytime soon on good ol' planet Earth.

CHAPTER ELEVEN

"THERE'S ABSOLUTELY NOTHING HERE."

The first night on Earth — but still aboard Mother — had passed without incident. Nobody slept right away. There was too much to talk about, things to go over and over. Finally, about three A.M. ship time, Jobs fell asleep. He dreamed of Cordelia, the girl he'd liked back on Earth. The girl whose death had been broadcast nationwide. In his dream he and Cordelia were in a playground, the old-fashioned kind with molded plastic ducks or tigers on short fat coils, close to the ground. Cordelia sat in a swing and Jobs pushed her higher, then higher, until the swing came down to meet his hands and the swing was empty. Jobs looked up and saw Cordelia floating away like a lost balloon, growing smaller and smaller. Then she was gone.

* * *

Day two.

Today they'd make the first of what would undoubtedly be many detailed explorations of the Shadow Zone. Jobs reviewed his mini-crew. He'd asked Mo'Steel to come along with them. Anamull, too. D-Caf had said yes reluctantly. And *big* surprise, Burroway had volunteered. Jobs couldn't figure out why. The man was definitely not the bravest.

Everyone still suffered symptoms of altitude sickness, or what Mo'Steel said was sometimes called acute mountain sickness back on old Earth. Mo'Steel, no triathlon winner but in the best physical shape, felt the least discomfort. D-Caf, still slightly pudgy in spite of everything he'd endured, was significantly worse off but determined to go back out.

"Ready, 'migo?" Mo'Steel stretched up onto his toes, fell back to flat feet.

Jobs nodded. "Let's go."

He led the others down the ramp.

Jobs looked out at a stretch of land about a quarter of a mile ahead that sort of looked like a fossilized, definitely postapocalyptic ruin of a city.

"Let's not go that way," Jobs said, pointing toward the rubble. "That can wait for another time. We'll just stay in this general area, and go a little farther

from the ship than we did last time. If you see anything interesting that's small enough for you to
carry, grab it and bring it back to the ship. It might
be something we can use later. You never know,
right?" Suddenly Jobs smiled a bit. "Oh, and I know I
sound like your mom or something, but don't forget
to wear your gloves. You know, in case of radiation
and all."

"Uh, professor? What do you mean by interesting?" Anamull asked.

"We're looking for any signs of life — vegeta-
tion, maybe even animal tracks. If, for some reason,
you find what looks like a human footprint, please
let me know. Other than that . . ." Jobs shrugged. "I
don't really know."

"Sounds okay to me," Mo'Steel said.

Burroway's face looked pained. He'd been com-
plaining of a headache since breakfast.

"Okay, spread out but make sure you can see the
rest of us."

Jobs and the others worked mostly without
speaking. Jobs sifted through the ash that covered
the ground in varying layers of thickness. He wondered what exactly the stuff was made of and made
sure to gather a good-sized scoop to take back to
the lab.

They worked in perpetual twilight. Breathing was difficult in the relatively thin atmosphere but Jobs felt his body adjusting. Already he felt less light-headed, less all-over achy than he had on and after the first expedition.

Jobs stretched and reached for his oxygen tank. As he breathed in the air, he realized that it was almost an hour since they'd begun the search and he still hadn't found one sign of life. He'd collected only ash, a few rocks.

He gestured for the group to gather.

"Anyone find anything?" he asked.

"There's absolutely nothing here," Burroway said disgustedly.

"D-Caf? Anything? Anamull?"

Both shook their heads.

"There's gotta be cockroaches," Mo'Steel said. "Nothing kills a roach. Not even a nuclear bomb."

"Well," Burroway sneered, "that's an encouraging thought." Jobs noted the man's chest rising and then falling heavily.

"What're you, afraid of roaches?" Anamull taunted.

D-Caf giggled, then choked for air.

Jobs knew they should probably go back to the ship soon. "Just a few more minutes," he said. He pointed to where he'd spotted a low rise in the land. "Over there."

Silently they agreed and began to walk toward the rise. They'd gone about three yards when . . .

WHOOSH!

"Whoa!" Mo'Steel stumbled back, into Jobs.

It was a pillar of flame. Jobs recognized the smell. Gas. It had shot out of the ground only two or three yards ahead.

"Okay," he mumbled, "something's definitely going on underground."

"We should get out of here," Burroway said, his voice high and frightened.

"I'm with you, man," Anamull agreed.

"Let's get going!" Jobs ordered. "Now."

We're not safe until we're on the ship, Jobs told himself. He'd seen no warning sign of the eruption. It could happen again at any moment, anywhere. . . . And what if the flaming gas erupted from beneath the ship itself?

The unsettling thought made him yell, "Run!" though everybody was running as best and as fast as they could.

Mo'Steel was out in front. Jobs and Burroway were roughly even, several steps behind. Anamull followed Jobs closely; D-Caf lagged.

If only we can . . .

WHOOSH!

Jobs's entire body stiffened with the suddenness of the explosion. He was momentarily blinded by a flash. He heard D-Caf and Anamull scream, then through foggy eyes saw Mo'Steel come to a stop, turn.

Burroway was gone. He was just — not there. Everything — his oxygen unit, his lead-lined speci-men bag — was no longer. The flaming gas had done its worst.

"Keep going!" Mo'Steel shouted, jolting Jobs back into motion. "Come on!"

A flame-retardant suit, Jobs thought as he ran. Yes, that's what he and Billy needed to make. He'd get to work on it right away, as soon as they got back to the ship.

If they got back to the ship.

(CHAPTER TWELVE)

"I'M NOT GOING OUT THERE."

"Only thirteen of us now." Olga shook her head, bit her lip.

Jobs was trying to get some of them to do some more exploring. But things were not going so well.

"Maybe we should just leave, just take off again," Noyze suggested.

2Face snorted. "Oh, yeah, that'll solve everything."

"It was just a suggestion!" Noyze snapped.

"No." Jobs looked at each person, one by one. "No. We're here now. We knew it would be hard. We knew we might . . . We knew maybe some people wouldn't make it. We really need to give this place a chance."

Jobs felt a tug at his sleeve. He looked down, saw nothing at first but the gray cafeteria wall, then the shape of a hand, realized it was his brother.

"Jobs, I'm scared and all, but if it helps, I'll go out there and spy and stuff, okay?"

"Thanks, Edward," Jobs said, touched. "Right now it looks like our biggest enemy is the environment and I don't know how to spy on that, but if we ever find any people . . ." The thought made Jobs feel suddenly very afraid. "If we ever need a spy," he went on shakily, "I'll be sure to let you know."

Roger Dodger shook his head. "I'm not going out there," he said. "No way. I don't want to burn up like Mr. Burroway. Uh-uh. Nope."

"I'll go," Anamull said. "It was seriously bad but, man, it beats hanging out with the nut job over here." Anamull jerked his thumb at Yago.

Yago smiled his spacey smile. "A prophet is never welcomed in his own home."

"I think it should be unanimous," Violet said suddenly. "I think every one of us should be in agreement about staying here on Earth until we learn more."

"A vote?" Jobs didn't know how to feel about Violet's suggestion.

Tate spoke up. "Whatever," she said. "I'll do whatever the majority wants to do."

"Oh, that's helpful." 2Face looked angry. "All right, you want a vote? I vote yes. We stay here at least until we determine if the planet is habitable. Correction. If the Shadow Zone, or whatever Jobs called it, is habitable. Olga?"

For a moment Olga didn't answer. Then she said, "Yes. I agree with 2Face. I vote yes."

"Me, too," Mo'Steel said.

They went around the room. Jobs listened to each "yes" or "okay" or "whatever" with slowly mounting excitement. Sure, Earth scared him. But it also intrigued him.

"Okay," 2Face declared. "It's unanimous. We stay."

Yago adjusted his grip on the upside-down-question-mark-like thing that was attached at the blunt end to an invisible power line in the basement's ceiling. *A ridiculous way to travel,* he thought. A monorail. So primitive. And undignified. When he was in charge, he'd have this entire basement revamped, upgraded. He'd put in a sophisticated shuttle system so he could ride anywhere throughout the ship in luxury and style.

Yago didn't care if anyone knew he was missing from the fortress. He had a larger, more important matter with which to concern himself.

He'd known that coming back to Earth was not

on his agenda. He'd only undertaken the brief foray to the surface to avoid unnecessary suspicion.

One look at the ugly, barren remains of Earth was enough for Yago to decide against hanging around longer than he had to. Anyone who thought they could pull a decent life out of that ash heap was wacko. And they had the nerve to call him crazy? Ha. Well, they'd learn soon enough. There was method to his madness. What he appeared to be and what he actually was were two very different things.

It was a bold move but Yago decided to take it. Alone. That cretin and the twitch, Anamull and D-Caf, had told him they wanted no part of him or his plan and that was fine with Yago. He didn't need them. He needed the Troika. And he was going to get them.

Yago recognized the approaching Dark Place from the time they'd met Amelia. The time some unenlightened Meanies had tried to arrest him.

The Dark Place was anything but. It appeared suddenly, a space of bright white light and very cool air Yago could feel yards away.

Yago loosened his grip and dropped neatly to the floor.

They were waiting for him.

"We meet again," Amelia said by way of greeting. She was as Yago remembered her. Long dark hair. Sparkling gray eyes. "You remember Charlie Langlow?" she said.

Oh, yeah, Yago thought. Mr. Porcupine. Yago offered his new greeting: "May you bask in the light of the truth."

"Uh-huh," Charlie grunted.

"And this is Duncan Choate," Amelia said, an amused smile on her face. "The third member of our group. The group you're so quaintly calling the Troika."

Yago experienced a flicker of jealousy. Duncan Choate was a good-looking guy. Maybe even better looking than Yago. But he just smiled and repeated his greeting with grace.

Yago promised not to let himself be annoyed by Amelia's condescension, Charlie's craziness, Duncan's looks. And he promised not to underestimate any one of them. He'd swallow his own ego — for the moment — and just figure out a way to deal with them. Pretend to accept their assertion of being more highly evolved than Yago and the others.

"You know everything that goes on aboard the ship," Yago said. "So you must know they're staying here, at least for now."

"We know," Amelia affirmed.

Duncan spoke softly. "Their innocence is fetching."

"I did not participate in their discussions," Yago went on. "You know that, too. What you don't know is that I have removed myself from them. I am no longer a part of that group."

Yago waited. It took Amelia only a second to understand what he was saying.

She grinned. "You're proposing an alliance with us? *You?* I'm not sure you aren't really insane."

"An alliance, yes," Yago said, unshaken by her mockery. "I want to gain control of the ship. I want your help and friendship."

Charlie crossed his arms over his chest defiantly. "What makes you think we'll work with you? What makes you think we *need* you?"

Duncan stayed quiet, though Yago was keenly aware of his stare.

"I believe we have the same agenda," Yago answered coolly. "At least, the same immediate goal. To regain control of the ship."

"To end Billy's control of the ship," Amelia said.

Yago nodded. Billy didn't matter to him one way or the other. "Whatever you say."

Amelia seemed to be considering his proposal. Yago watched her glance intently at Charlie, then at

Duncan. He wondered if they were communicating in some way he couldn't see or hear.

Finally, she looked back to Yago. There was a glint of amusement in her eyes. "Okay," she said. "We'll talk. What exactly did you have in mind?"

CHAPTER THIRTEEN

". . . NOW YOU'RE THE BIGGEST FREAK OF ALL."

Tate's eyes popped open. She was completely awake. Around her, others slept. She identified Olga's slight snore, Violet's sigh. The room was dark and still.

Tate sat up, all senses alert. Yes . . . there it was. A sound. A footstep? A memory of her mother came into her head then, of her mother appearing at Tate's cribside almost before she'd begun to cry. Tate shook off the memory, focused on the strange sound. She crept out of her bed, snuck out of the room.

It was "night" on the ship. No one was supposed to be walking around the dorm. You were supposed to be asleep — at least in bed — or at your station. Someone was breaking curfew.

Or . . . Tate swallowed hard. Or maybe the sound she'd heard had come from a Meanie or a Rider who'd broken through the shields and snuck past the other Remnants. If that was the case, Tate knew there'd be serious trouble.

Tate let her eyes adjust to the semidarkness of the corridor. She stiffened. There it was again — there *they* were. Definitely footsteps, off to the left, down the corridor, moving toward the guys' room. Cautiously, Tate advanced in the direction of the footsteps, keeping her back against the wall, eyes wide.

And then . . .

She saw him, identified him, translated him into Enemy in a semiconscious second.

He was Threat.

He was Harm.

He was Betrayal.

Tate felt herself slipping away. Something was happening. She didn't know what was happening except that it wasn't stopping. She was seeing in red, everything in red. Even her skin, all bright red in the dim corridor. And brighter than everything else, the Enemy.

She had changed.

She surged forward.

She was big and powerful.

She was efficient.

It began.

Through the bright hot frenzy came a voice. Shrill, frantic.

Tate stumbled, felt for the wall. Through a pinkish mist she saw Yago on the ground. His head and shoulders and upper arms were full of what looked like *bite marks*. He was breathing heavily, gasping for air.

Jobs was there, too, kneeling by Yago. And 2Face. And Anamull.

"What happened? I . . . I can't remember. . . ." Tate put her hands to her head, blinked.

"You were biting Yago," Anamull said, his voice rushed and awed. "You were, like, some huge bear or something with an even bigger mouth. We heard him screaming."

"Another minute and he would have suffocated," Jobs said, his voice tight.

"Why did you attack him?" 2Face asked, her good eye narrowed in suspicion.

Tate was overcome by guilt. Yago — he was weird and could be cruel but he was one of theirs, not the enemy.

Tate was filled with self-revulsion. She looked down warily at her stomach. There were no obvious bumps or odd bulges, nothing. She wondered if she'd actually swallowed anything. The thought made her stomach heave.

"Well," 2Face said as Tate tried to get her stomach under control, "now you're the biggest freak of all."

Duncan Choate sat in a classic meditation pose, legs crossed, feet resting on his thighs, hands resting there, too, palms upward, back straight, eyes half-closed. He liked to sit like this, sometimes for hours, thinking or dreaming or tuning in to the lives of the humans on board the ship. Back before the Rock, back when Duncan was only a child, he'd learned to integrate meditation into his daily routine. Reflection was as important as action. Besides, stress was very bad for the complexion.

Duncan started to think about Yago.

They were alike in some ways. Correction. They'd been somewhat alike back on Earth, before the Rock. Duncan ran down the list. Both extremely good-looking and very well aware of it. Nothing wrong with being honest. Both unashamedly self-focused, some would say — had said — self-centered. Again, nothing wrong with looking out for number one. The big difference, though, as Duncan saw it, was that back when they were both "old-fashioned"

humans, Duncan had been hardworking, intellectu-
ally sharp, ambitious. Yago, on the other hand, had
been essentially lazy. Sure, Yago wanted big things
for himself; he just wanted someone else to get
them for him. Duncan wanted big things for himself
and wanted to get them all by himself. And he had.

When the call came about his berth on the
Mayflower, Duncan had been a twenty-year-old bio-
engineering student at MIT. Full academic scholarship. Major job offers already, though Duncan was
only a sophomore and had at least six more years of
formal education ahead of him. He was the kind of
guy who just couldn't get less than an A, one hundred percent, glowing personal recommendations.
Early on, Duncan had come to accept the simple fact
that he was a likable genius.

And just as early on, Duncan had accepted the
fact that he was also a damned good athlete. For
whatever reason, cycling had most captured his interest.

For a while he'd seriously considered doing the
Tour de France, maybe going on to the Olympics.
Spend a few years perfecting the physical and men-
tal skills of a world-class athlete. Then he'd come
back to MIT if he liked, pick up where he left off,
catch up on all the new advances in his field. He'd

still have a scholarship. He'd still have job offers. He could still write his own ticket. Duncan was nothing if not calmly self-assured.

Well, the Rock had messed that all up, all his plans. The Rock had taken his life out of his own control and for an in-charge, superorganized, careful planner like Duncan, that was a huge blow.

But then something had happened he'd never imagined — something he still didn't fully under- stand — and the result was that Duncan Choate had bypassed basic organic evolution and in an in- credibly short period of time become a superevolved being. Amelia and Charlie Langlow he couldn't speak for. But Duncan Choate knew that Duncan Choate deserved everything he had gotten and more.

Duncan closed his eyes completely, went inside, slowed his rate of respiration, saw Yago. Interest- ingly, Yago was also "special," far further along the evolutionary path than the ordinary humans on board the ship. Yago had the Touch.

Duncan wasn't sure he liked Yago. He was ab- solutely sure he didn't trust him. But he was in no way afraid of him. He knew all about pre-Rock Yago, the badly spoiled son of the President of the United States of America. He knew all about — had wit- nessed — Yago's trip with Mother, his being made "president," his forced march against the Children as head of a bizarre reincarnation of a Union battalion from the U.S. Civil War. He knew all about Yago's "death" in battle. There was no doubt in Duncan's prodigious mind that Yago was mostly insane.

But there was also the matter of the Touch, the sensation the Meanies — a faction of them, anyway — couldn't seem to do without.

Just how evolved was Yago? Who was winning the race, Yago or Duncan? Duncan couldn't be sure, yet. But he would be. And in the meantime, he'd have some fun with his new partner in crime.

Duncan opened his eyes, smiled. Once Yago got over the trauma of being that girl's midnight snack.

(CHAPTER FOURTEEN)

A BIZARRE TREASURE HUNT.

Fourth time away from the ship. This time they were going into the city. There was a "beyond the city," Jobs knew that, but for now, one step at a time. They still had the random pillars of flame to deal with. And a fire extinguisher wasn't going to do much good — it would be like trying to cool yourself with an ice cube. Useless. And who knew what other nasty surprises awaited them.

Mo'Steel and 2Face had stayed on board with Billy. And with Yago, of course, who still refused to set foot on Earth after his first, brief visit. Since the ship's landing Yago had been withdrawn; after the first, introductory excursion he'd kept to himself, spent a lot of time sitting perfectly still and staring into the middle distance. When he wasn't pacing a hallway, babbling to himself. Jobs couldn't deny he liked Yago better this way, *out* of the way.

So this group consisted of Olga, Violet, Edward, Noyze, Roger Dodger — a surprise volunteer — Anamull, D-Caf, and Tate.

It took them almost an hour with their slightly goofy, low-gravity stride to reach the edge of the city.

It was a fantastical place, a place that in some macabre way appealed to Jobs's poetic sensibility. It reminded him of every movie he'd ever seen about a postapocalyptic Earth. It was every in-the-dismal-future piece of science fiction he'd ever read. It was every bombed-out city in every deadly war. And yet, it was none of those; it was completely unique.

Stairs led nowhere. Bridges spanned nothing, ended in midair. Doorways opened onto emptiness. Windows overlooked rubble. All that remained were suggestions of a world. Reminders of a life. Piles of refuse all dull black and bone white and dirty gray.

"What, no welcoming committee? No keys to the city?" Olga quipped feebly.

"Guess we really are out-of-towners," Violet said.

"Right," Jobs said. "We're strangers. This is a strange place. Be careful. We don't know the rules."

Tate grunted. "Just observe, don't interfere? Who's going to care either way? Let's just get this over with."

*   *   *

They'd spread out within an area small enough to allow each person to be seen or heard by at least one other person.

"Hey, look at this!" Roger Dodger called. "It's some sort of cool fossil."

Tate watched him clamber over a tumble of rock.

"Let me see," Olga said, holding out her gloved hand.

"What is it?" Tate peered at the object, wondering.

Olga turned the object over and around. Her face assumed a pained and, at the same time, tender expression. "It's a bone fragment," she said, handing it back to Roger Dodger. "From a small dog, I think."

Roger Dodger's face fell. "Oh."

"This place is nothing more than a burned-out mess," Tate said irritably. "It's too depressing."

Tate watched as Roger Dodger tossed the fragment onto a heap of ash and ambled away. She hoped the next souvenir he found would be less gruesome.

The kid had been convinced to come along when she promised to look out for him. Tate was still seriously disgusted by her mutation. It gave a whole new meaning to the term "deadly virus." A whole new level to the notion of an eating disorder.

But Tate supposed it could be a good thing if she could learn to control it and not attack people on her own side of the conflict. For example, if some creature here on Earth threatened Roger Dodger, she could keep her promise of protecting him by morphing the Mouth.

Of course, maybe there was no controlling the Mouth. Maybe it was in total control of her.

Jobs walked among the group as they searched and gathered. *A bizarre treasure hunt,* he thought. An amusement park for the terminally melancholy. The ultimate ghost town. Jobs knew he was imagining it but he swore he could smell the city burning — still.

Jobs watched as Tate unearthed a twisted piece of metal that D-Caf thought was a car fender and that Anamull insisted was some part of a subway car. "It's nothing," Tate snapped. "It's junk." She tossed the metal away from her, moved on.

Jobs moved on, too. He wondered how many of them knew about Tate's new mutation. He doubted she'd told anyone, though Anamull had probably blabbed to everyone. Either way, since the night she'd attacked Yago, Tate had been on edge. Jobs guessed she was afraid of herself. He felt bad but didn't know what he could do about it.

Jobs spotted D-Caf peering at something he held in his hand. "What is it?" Jobs asked.

D-Caf shrugged. "I'm not sure but — I think it's a 2011 model, state-of-the-art handheld link."

Jobs smiled. "You can tell all that just by looking at a black lump?"

"Yeah. It doesn't work, of course."

"Right." Jobs walked on.

Something that looked like the ravaged inside of a baseball lifted off the ground, stopped about three or four feet in the air. Jobs looked hard. It was Edward, picking up an artifact, examining it.

He's an orphan. A scavenger.

And so am I.

(CHAPTER FIFTEEN)

"IT'S WORTH SOMETHING TO ME."

"Oh, wow, look at this!" Violet exclaimed. In her hands she held a blackened, vaguely rectangular box, without its lid. "It's a blow-pen set," she told Jobs. "I'd completely forgotten about these things. They were for little kids." Violet paused, eyeing Jobs mischievously. "And I never liked the idea of of creating a painting with your mouth. Why not just paint a painting the good old-fashioned way?"

Jobs didn't have a witty response. "Strange," he said, half to himself, "what didn't get completely smashed. Why didn't a bunch of plastic pens in a plastic case just melt? It's so weird. It makes you wonder. . . ."

"What?" Violet looked back up from the pen set.

"Well, it makes you wonder if any people survived. I mean, if a plastic toy got through intact, maybe some people did, too," Jobs said, feeling the excitement rise in his voice. "If they prepared for the Rock by building some sort of underground bunker —"

"Or if they were just lucky," Violet interrupted. "If it's lucky to live through the destruction of the world as you know it."

Suddenly, Jobs felt deflated. "That's what we've done, isn't it? And I don't feel very lucky," he admitted.

Noyze had found a fragment of a china dinner plate, all flowery and pastel. Jobs saw her put it in her lead-lined bag.

"I don't think that's worth anything to us," he said.

"It's worth something to me!" Noyze replied fiercely. "My grandmother had a set of china with a pattern almost like that. She used her fancy dishes on Sundays. My parents and me, we had dinner at Grandma's every Sunday. Roast beef and carrots with maple syrup sauce and mashed potatoes. The lumpy kind because my dad liked them that way."

Jobs blushed and said, "Oh."

Again, he moved on.

Jobs stuck the tip of a special probe he'd constructed into the ashy ground. The device was intended to register any signs of radio waves. They'd listened for radio waves from the ship and come up empty, but Jobs was nothing if not persistent. Something could be going on under the earth's surface. Something had to be. Jobs tightened his concentration.

Nothing. Jobs pulled the probe from the ground, chose another spot about a yard away, repeated the process.

Still nothing.

He kept going.

Violet stood, transfixed.

There were four figures, roughly the same size. They sat cross-legged, one on each side of a low square table a little over a foot from the ground. Under the table was a smallish melted appliance with the remains of a cord extending from its base. Violet guessed it had been an electric heater.

Walls were long gone, as was a ceiling. The figures appeared as if on display at a museum.

"They're like stone." Violet turned and saw that Olga had joined her. Her eyes were wide with fascination.

"Like those people from Pompeii," Violet murmured. "When the volcano erupted. Vesuvius. These people must have just flash-frozen somehow."

Olga hung back while Violet stepped closer, carefully, and examined each detail of the eerie scene. The floor was covered by a tatami mat. *Correction*, Violet noted. The floor was now the tatami mat itself, floor and mat having fused together. On the table — melded to its surface — a small rectangular dish, a tiny cup, a pair of chopsticks, and a medium-sized bowl sat before each of the seated figures. They were like simple clay figures fired in a kiln.

"I think they are — they were — Japanese," Violet said suddenly. "I can tell from the utensils, the tatami mat. Now it makes sense. There are no remaining environmental features, no mountains, lakes, and all but . . . Olga, did you see . . . Well, I'll show you, come on."

Violet grabbed Olga's arm and talked excitedly as they made their way through a world of debris. "There's a structure over here on the ground, of course, broken up, but something about it made me flash on the Eiffel Tower. And then I thought, oh, yeah, the Tokyo Tower in Tokyo. It kind of looked like the Eiffel Tower. I saw it on a business trip I took with my mother." Violet stopped abruptly, turned to face her companion. "Olga, I think this area was Tokyo."

"I just assumed it would be America," Olga admitted. "Pretty silly. What difference would it have made?"

"None," Violet said unnecessarily. She thought about the grim tableau, four lonely figures at a table. "The whole world was wiped out."

Jobs heard it before he saw it. A loud, slow rumbling. In seconds it grew to a louder, more rapid rumbling. Jobs whirled, tried to locate the source of the noise. Then — a crash, the tumbling of stone, and a scream.

"Help! Somebody help!"

Jobs raced toward the panicked voice, toward the billow of what looked like smoke but wasn't. It was just air, thick with stone dust and disturbed ash.

"Help her!" Roger Dodger pointed at the ground. Noyze was sprawled, leaning up on her elbows, captured under a long, tubular piece of metal or wood. Hard to tell at first glance.

Together, Anamull and D-Caf heaved the rotted beam off Noyze's right leg.

"Thanks," Noyze whispered.

Roger Dodger was frantic. "She was climbing and I was going to catch her if she fell but . . ."

"Shhh! It's not your fault," Olga assured him. "Let me take a look at this."

Olga knelt in the ash and made a quick examination of Noyze's leg.

"Is it broken?" Noyze gasped.

"No. I don't think so. Just cut up some, and you're going to be covered in bruises by morning."

Noyze smiled shakily. "That's good. That it's not broken, I mean."

"What were you trying to do, anyway?" Tate asked, putting her arm around Roger Dodger's shoulders.

"Read an inscription. Look. That stone over there. It fell. It was at the top of this — whatever this is. Help me over to it?"

Olga frowned. "Well, all right. But then we're calling it a day."

Jobs nodded. "Olga's right. We've seen enough."

Tate slung Noyze's right arm around her shoulder; Jobs took the left. Together they helped her hop to the fallen stone.

Jobs watched as, with fingers and mind, using all of her formidable language skills, Noyze examined the heavily damaged stone. After a moment she said, "It's in English and Japanese." Noyze worked on. "This stone was part of a monument to the Japanese people who perished at Hiroshima and Nagasaki," she said, clearly absorbed in the excitement of deciphering. "Not all of the inscription is left. I can feel one complete line, though."

"What does it say?" Jobs asked.

"It says: *From the people of the United States of America, dedicated in the year 2008.*"

There was silence. Jobs felt depression begin to press on his skull and fought it. He watched expressions darken and harden. What else was there to do? Smile? Say, "Wow"?

"Let's get going," he said loudly, startling himself, turning to lead the way back to the ship.

(CHAPTER SIXTEEN)

JOBS WAS LEAVING THE SHIP.

Jobs glanced at the clock, saw it was past midnight, ship time. With some reluctance he began to clear away his equipment for the night, brought test tubes to the lab sink, rinsed them, then put them in the sterilizer.

As he worked he felt the now familiar mood settling over him. He knew he'd lost the race but felt compelled to finish it. That's why he'd taken a handful of seeds from the tomatoes available in the dining area, enhanced them with doses of vitamins and enzymes and minerals. That's why he'd taken a quantity of ash from the surface and cleared it as best he knew how of traces of radioactivity.

The night before, Jobs had planted the seeds in a pot of clean ash and doused them with purified water. The plan now was to transplant them — in the pot — to Earth's surface. See what would happen in the open air.

He knew nothing would actually grow from the seeds. First of all, the tomato seeds weren't even really seeds — just copies. *Face it,* he told himself again. *Life didn't spring from nothing.* At least not in a simple, one-step biological sense. But he was going to plant the seeds anyway.

Jobs gathered what he'd need and left the lab. For a moment he felt overwhelmingly like Jack in the old fairy tale "Jack and the Beanstalk." Everybody thought Jack was a fool until he proved them otherwise. The thought made Jobs smile. Maybe he was a fool, but sometimes somebody needed to have the nerve to be one. He just hoped he didn't run into a people-eating giant.

Jobs stepped on the elevator that would bring him to the basement, vaguely aware that he was breaking curfew. Aware that he was about to break the agreement not to leave the ship alone.

Knowing he had no choice but to fight his depression with action.

From his secret observation post in a small, unused room adjacent to the lab, Yago watched Jobs leave.

Perfect. Yago nodded with satisfaction. He'd made an accurate assessment of Jobs. He'd known Jobs wouldn't give up, knew he'd attempt the improbable.

Yago followed Jobs down a long hallway, under a towering arch, past walls of smooth dull metal, through the attic's massive entrance hall, topped by a transparent dome. There was no sign of Billy, of anyone. With Duncan's help, Yago had made sure the others were given an undetectable dose of a deep relaxant in their evening meal.

Down the elevator to the base of the fortress, Yago continued to follow Jobs.

Jobs was leaving the ship. Yago watched him punch in a code on the keypad next to the door. He watched the door slide open, the ramp lower. Jobs stepped out onto the ramp, walked, activated a mechanism at the bottom of the ramp that would close the ship's door but allow the ramp to remain in place. As soon as Jobs had started off into the constant twilight, Yago hurried forward and punched in the code to stop the door from closing. He peered into the gloom and motioned for Yago's Formidable Intellect, hidden behind an abutment of the ship. He then instructed the Meanie to follow farther and observe Jobs's actions.

"I'll be waiting for your report," he added softly. "If it's satisfactory . . ."

Yago's Formidable Intellect gestured eagerly.

"Yes. You will be rewarded."

Yago backed into the ship, reactivated the door, and went to bed.

(CHAPTER SEVENTEEN)

"WE CAN'T TURN ON ONE ANOTHER NOW."

"You know, these meetings are such a colossal waste of time," Tate grumbled.

"Normally, I'd agree with you," Olga said. "But I don't see that we have much choice right now."

They were gathered in the common dining area, some standing with arms folded, others straddling chairs, others leaning against the cafeteria-style tables.

They were debating their next move. Jobs felt his stomach flutter.

"What about a longer-range expedition?" he said, trying to keep the panic out of his voice. They couldn't just leave Earth now. They *couldn't*. "Billy and I can develop a land vehicle that —"

"No way," Violet said. "I'm not going out of sight of the ship. I could get burned to death by a flaming pillar of gas just by taking one step off the ship's ramp."

"I'd go," Jobs said. "I'd ask for one volunteer to go with me. That's all. The rest of you can stay on the ship where it's safe."

Tate snorted. "Safe? You've forgotten about the Meanies and the Riders and the Troika?"

Jobs let it go. "There's got to be something here," he insisted. "Something we've missed."

"Who are you trying to convince, Duck?" Mo'Steel said.

Jobs was startled. "What?"

"That's a real question," Mo'Steel said, and he wasn't smiling. "I mean, if it comes down to it, I'll support you all the way 'cause you're my bud and you're the smartest person I know. But I gotta be honest. I'm not getting a good vibe off our hanging around."

Jobs felt oddly embarrassed. "No. Of course. I know. But I still think . . ."

Violet laughed. "That's Jobs, always thinking. Look," she said, gesturing at him with her four-fingered hand, "if you hadn't told everyone about finding Earth, none of this would be happening. We wouldn't have broken the Big Compromise. Life wasn't perfect but it was okay. More than okay. Why couldn't you have just kept your big mouth shut?"

Jobs felt as though he'd been dealt a physical

blow. He tried to answer, to defend himself some-how, but the words wouldn't come.

"But the Meanies attacked you, Violet!" Edward countered. "I was there. They broke the Big Compromise, not Jobs."

Jobs thought how odd and unfair it was for his little brother to be arguing so angrily with older kids and adults. It made him feel bad.

2Face jumped in angrily. "Look, I'm not defending them, but the Meanies only broke the Big Compromise because Yago interfered in their lives. If anyone's really to blame here, it's Yago."

"Right! You were the one who talked us into turning the ship around," Noyze cried. "You went to Billy on your own. You didn't even wait for Jobs and Mo'Steel and the rest of them to come back from the basement so they could vote."

"I didn't see anyone trying to stop me," 2Face shot back.

D-Caf's face was flushed. "We . . . ah, we were in shock over what had happened to Violet and T.R.," he said hesitantly. "At least, I was."

"Yeah, 'cause you're a wimp," Anamull sneered. "A whining little —"

"Stop!" Olga cried. "All of you, do you see what we're doing? We're blaming one another, yelling, call-

LOST AND FOUND

ing one another names. This is totally unreasonable.
We can't turn on one another now. We'll never survive unless we stick together."

There was a moment of awkward silence. Jobs
thought he might faint; the rush of anger and frustration had made him feel sick. Then Noyze spoke.

"Look, Olga's right," she conceded. "Fighting is
getting us nowhere. Besides, it's not like we're on a
rescue mission. It's not like the Rock just happened
and if we try hard enough we're going to dig out
survivors. It's been five hundred years. So . . . I'm
sorry for letting my anger get out of control."

2Face still glowered but shrugged. "Me, too."

"I'm sorry, Jobs," Violet said, turning to him, eyes
bright with tears. "I'm sorry, everyone."

Jobs shook his head, said, "It's okay." But inside
he wasn't really sure it was.

CHAPTER EIGHTEEN

"AMAZING, ISN'T IT?"

Yago and Duncan were in the back of the huge, sparse basement of the ship. The others were having a meeting up on the bridge, a meeting Yago wanted no part of. He was fine without them. Besides, Duncan had bugged the bridge so if anything important was decided in the meeting, anything that might affect their plan, Yago and the Troika would know. Of course, Duncan had pointed out that he could hear the meeting just fine without a bug, but since Yago couldn't . . .

Yago didn't like his supposed weaknesses pointed out to him. Who did Duncan think he was? Obviously, he didn't realize just how great Yago was.

But that's not really his fault, is it? Yago thought. An idea began to form. *I haven't taken the time to show him,* he admitted. *Well, now is the time.*

Duncan's eyes were closed. Yago knew he was

somewhere else on the ship, probably at the meeting.

"Duncan!" he said loudly.

Slowly, Duncan opened his eyes. Yago got a strange mix of emotions off Duncan, contempt and amusement along with genuine affection. Back on Earth, Yago had never had a real friend, never felt the need for one, was contemptuous of emotional relationships. Now, something about Duncan . . . Sometimes Yago felt that he and Duncan were actually becoming friends. Then he'd catch something snake-like in Duncan's expression and feel that Duncan was just playing with him, pretending to — what? Like him? Duncan confused Yago.

"It is time," he said. "Time for you to see the True Path. Time for you to join the ranks. Time for you to come to know The One."

Duncan put a hand to his chest, bowed his head. "But Great One, I feel so unworthy!"

"You are," Yago snapped.

Duncan shrugged slightly, lowered his hand, raised his head.

Yago never even had to think about what he was doing when he bestowed the Touch on his Meanies. But now, with a human, or whatever Duncan was, Yago found himself concentrating, willing the Touch to work its magic. He would bestow a great gift upon Duncan Choate, something he would never forget.

Yago called to himself a mantle of serenity and power and pride. He straightened his spine, looked deep in Duncan's eyes, extended his hand. Gently he placed his hand on Duncan's forearm.

Yago waited. Nothing happened. Duncan didn't move. His eyes didn't roll back in his head, his breathing didn't quicken.

Yago tried harder. He willed the Touch to work, he called up every bit of his incredible power. . . .

"Sorry, Yago." Duncan's voice was falsely sympathetic. He took Yago's hand, removed it from his own arm. "Does nothing for me. Nada. Zero. You lose."

Yago felt rage rear up in him. *It isn't my fault,* he told himself. *It's Duncan's fault. Duncan is unworthy.* Duncan looked at him just then with a funny expression on his face and Yago got the creepy feeling Duncan had read his mind.

"Now it's my turn," Duncan said. "Let me show you something really spectacular."

Yago took a step away from Duncan. He found himself suddenly trembling and afraid.

Duncan turned to allow Yago a view of his back. Instantly, Duncan's shirt ripped open and from his spine sprouted what had to be ancillary brains. Yago knew what a human brain looked like and these four — things — were brains all right, stems attached to one thick spinal cord, its bulge visible through the skin and bone.

Yago pressed a hand over his mouth, revolted. What happened next was even worse.

Duncan continued to smile serenely as an arm sprang from just beneath his original right arm, another from just beneath his original left. Duncan had four arms. His shirt was gone now, hanging in shreds. Yago blinked, saw with horror that two more limbs were stretching to life from Duncan's bare chest.

And then . . . flesh and bone and muscle forced themselves through Duncan's jeans, formed a sort of horizontal shelf, then dropped vertically to form another set of legs and feet. Again, the same thing, yet another set of legs grew from the secondary set. Duncan's body now extended at least a yard from left to right.

Yago moaned. Duncan was like a perversion of one of those statues from India, Yago didn't know which, but the ones with like twenty arms and twenty legs, all wiggling and undulating at once, the face blandly serene and smiling.

Yago couldn't see how all those limbs could fit on one human body, but they did. He knew he was seeing the impossible but he believed it to be true. After all the months on board this psycho ship, how could he not?

Duncan was a carnival sideshow attraction. *He has Lobster Boy beat by miles,* Yago thought, feeling sick to his stomach.

"Amazing, isn't it?" Duncan said. "Though I do ruin a lot of clothes."

"What do you . . . uh, do?" Yago said, failing to keep the quiver out of his voice. There had to be a point to this . . . monstrosity.

Duncan laughed. "I am the Über-multitasker, the Ultimate Can-doer, the Supreme Solution to your busy life. Allow me to demonstrate."

Yago wanted to protest that he didn't need a demonstration but the words got stuck in his throat. Could anything he'd say stop Duncan now, anyway?

Yago watched, transfixed, as Duncan's two original hands tied elaborate sailor's knots in lengths of rope — where had the rope come from? Duncan's hands were empty, but now they held rope.

With another hand/brain Duncan produced a pen and paper and set to work, "calculating the distance between the base of the elevator and the basement," he explained, and found the answer in less than thirty seconds of scribbling. Yago assumed it was the right answer; he couldn't even begin to do the math.

Another set of hands spoke what Yago recognized as American Sign Language. "I'm reciting Shakespeare. *Romeo and Juliet*," Duncan said. Those words came out of his mouth but who knew what monstrous tumorlike brain was behind them. Yago cringed even thinking about it.

One set of Duncan's legs/feet kept a soccer ball in play. *Where had that come from?* Yago thought. His mind spun. Rope and a soccer ball and pen and paper . . . Whatever props Duncan needed for his macabre exhibition seemed to just appear. *Maybe it's all a trick,* Yago thought, *an illusion.* Duncan was nothing more than a magician, okay, good enough for Las Vegas if Vegas were still around, better even than Harry Houdini or David Blaine with the help of an assistant and cameras, but . . .

Yago swallowed hard. Duncan was looking at him again with that funny expression Yago recognized from before. Without a doubt Yago knew Duncan had read his thoughts.

In a flash, one of the arms extending from Duncan's chest seemed to shoot out of its socket — if it had one — and zoom at Yago like a snake popping out of a can. Yago screamed and the hand grasped him around the middle, lifted him off the floor as if he were a tiny plastic action figure. The arm had doubled in length; the fingers had grown long enough to entirely encompass Yago's waist.

"Put me down!" Yago screamed.

"In a minute. I need to get some exercise." Duncan's grin widened as he straightened his elbow, lowering Yago almost to the floor, then lifting him to shoulder height, then raising him above his head. "You're a little light to be much use in serious weight training, but . . ."

"Why are you doing this?" Yago whimpered. His head swam; he closed his eyes but that made it worse. He desperately hoped he wouldn't throw up.

"Got to keep the mind and body in good shape," Duncan answered easily. "No point in neglecting one or the other."

And then Duncan began to run, many feet slapping down on the basement floor, faster and faster. "The minute mile," Yago heard Duncan say as Yago's vision became one dark blur.

Yago thought he must have passed out. Because suddenly he was on the floor, on his hands and knees, gasping, trying to stop the world from spinning out of control.

Slowly, carefully, he raised his head, sat back on his haunches. Duncan, clothes in tatters, lounged against a thick column, examining his fingernails. There were only ten of them. Duncan had only two arms, two legs. He saw Yago looking at him, twisted, showed Yago his normal back.

"Interesting, isn't it?" he drawled.

Yago heaved himself to his feet. He had no answer so he told himself it was best to say nothing. *Anything you say can and will be used against you . . .* Yago thought inanely.

Duncan pushed himself away from the column, opened his mouth to speak.

"Shut up! Listen!" Yago commanded. The bug Duncan had placed in the dining area was doing its job. How, Yago didn't know. In the end it didn't matter. As long as it worked, allowed Yago to hear.

Vaguely, since coming down to the basement, Yago had been aware of the voices, low and murmuring, even though he hadn't been able to identify a particular place from which they were coming. Then Duncan had gone berserk and Yago had been too crazed with fear to hear anything but the rapid beating of his own stressed heart. Now . . . It was too good to be true. The voices were all around him, harsh and loud and angry. People were divided, arguing, speaking without reason.

He heard someone say, "If we don't find some sign of life in the next twenty-four hours . . ." Olga?

Yago turned back to Duncan, grinned. He'd heard enough to make him feel slightly mollified after his embarrassing failure to move Duncan with the Touch. And after Duncan's show-off performance. At least things with the Remnants were going just as he'd hoped.

CHAPTER NINETEEN

JUST DEAL WITH IT.

They stood as if at attention, muscles rigid, heart rates synchronized, eyes wide and blank.

"The Ancient Enemy is among us," Charlie intoned.

Duncan picked up the chant. "We are the Ancient Enemy."

"The Ancient Enemy is among us." Amelia's voice was deep and ecstatic. "We are the Ancient Enemy."

The Troika joined minds. They spoke as one.

"The Ancient Enemy is all."

Yago gave the order.

Yago's Formidable Intellect slipped off to do Yago's bidding. He'd told Yago he was honored to have been chosen for such a deed. Yago had rewarded him with the Touch, then gone into the common dining area for a snack.

The room was empty except for Anamull sitting at the far end of a table, hunched over a bowl of gross chili. He chose a bright red apple from the large fruit bowl on a side table — Billy couldn't seem to manufacture green or yellow apples, and forget about anything exotic like a mango — and bit into it. *A little grainy,* he thought. Note to self: When in charge of ship, improve daily menu.

Yago caught Anamull watching him and made sure his mask of blankness was in place. Very, very slowly he walked from the dining area, making sure to stumble slightly. Behind him he heard Anamull grunt in amusement.

Soon, very soon, Yago would be in control of the ship. No more slobs like that brute back there. After that, he'd eliminate the Troika, somehow, some way. Yago didn't stop to think that perhaps they were reading his mind at that moment. He was too caught up in his own grandeur.

But for the moment, he'd concentrate on the now. And on Jobs. *It was like taking candy from a baby,* Yago thought, daze-walking to the sleeping area. It was so easy to fool someone who wanted something so badly. Their wanting made their judgment weak, took away their reasoning.

Jobs wanted life on Earth? "Well, then," Yago

whispered to no one, hoped someone saw him talking to himself, "he's certainly going to get it."

The mood was dismal. The plan was for Mother to lift off in four hours' time, get back out on some as-yet-undetermined course. No one had wanted to waste time investigating the two smaller chunks of Earth. Well, Jobs had wanted to but he was alone in his vote. How could they "waste time," he thought, when time was all they had? No specific place to go, no one waiting for them to show up . . .

We've failed, Jobs thought. *I've failed.* He wasn't even sure why they were going on this final trip. They weren't going to find anything because there was nothing to find. Earth was uninhabitable. *Deal with it,* Jobs told himself. *Just deal with it.*

Everybody was on the surface except for 2Face and Billy. And Yago, of course. It was as if most of those who'd hated Earth from the landing wanted one last look at what had once been their home. A very, very long time ago.

And that's all some of them were doing, Jobs noted. Looking. Saying good-bye. Anamull squinted off in the direction of the Bright Zone, kicked the ashy dust at his feet. Roger Dodger followed Tate like a shadow, hanging over her as she squatted and lazily poked at the ground with a small shovel. D-Caf seemed fascinated with a hangnail on his thumb. Violet stood, head down, arms folded. She seemed deep in thought and Jobs felt a sharp pang of loss. Since Violet had discovered her mutation she'd pulled away from him, withdrawn from their friendship. And everything that had happened since, from 2Face's trickery to Jobs's own failure to fully reveal information about Earth, had further alienated Jobs from his friend. He doubted they'd ever recapture what they'd once had between them.

What's the point of standing around? Jobs thought angrily and opened his mouth to call an end to it all.

"Jobs!" someone shouted. "Jobs, over here!"

CHAPTER TWENTY

"IS IT REAL?"

It was Noyze. She was crouching, leg still bandaged over the worst injuries, just where Jobs had planted those pitiful seeds.

Jobs bounded over, his mind refusing to acknowledge the slim possibility of . . .

Noyze scooted aside to let Jobs kneel close to the spot at which she pointed. "Look, Jobs. It's . . . I think it's alive."

Jobs put his weight on his hand, leaned close to the ground. His lips were set against any undue emotion. *Stay calm,* he told himself. *Just be cool.* He felt a minuscule bit of salty water course halfway down his cheek.

"Jobs?" It was Mo'Steel, crouching next to him. Vaguely, Jobs was aware that the others had come to see whatever it was he was staring at. They stood around him, peering over his shoulder, leaning close.

It's a joke, Jobs thought. *Has to be. Or maybe it's a natural mistake, the one and only of its kind.* He looked again. It was a seedling, nothing more but nothing less. It was slim and stood about three inches off the ground. Its stem was brownish; the three leaves were a dark, dull green. *Jack and the Beanstalk,* Jobs thought, and almost giggled.

"Oh, no way." That was Tate. "I don't believe it. Can it . . . Is it real?"

Jobs shook his head. "I don't know," he said, voice trembling. "I planted some seeds the other night. I . . . they're not . . . I never thought . . . I didn't dare to think anything would grow. I'm still not sure anything really did."

"What do you mean?" Noyze said excitedly. "Look at it! It's alive."

"It seems to be," Jobs countered.

"Should I touch it, Duck?"

Jobs leaned back a bit, considered. "I don't know," he admitted. "It could be contaminated, though I sterilized what I could."

Mo'Steel got down flat on his stomach, inched forward on the ashy ground. "I'm going to smell it."

He did, turned to Jobs, grinned. "Smells very faintly like basil."

Jobs shook his head. "No. I planted tomato seeds."

He felt a hand on his shoulder. "Let me try," Olga said. "I know my herbs."

Olga scooted close to the seedling, sniffed, scooted back. "Definitely basil. I mean, its smell is similar. But I don't think we're going to be making a salad anytime soon."

Jobs continued to kneel on the ashy ground. His rational mind didn't seem able to function. Instead, mind and body were flooded with waves of emotion. Jobs felt massive disbelief followed so closely by suspicion he didn't know where one stopped and the other started. Suspicion was followed closely by caution, which metamorphosed slowly, unbelievably into excitement.

What if this is real? Jobs thought, feeling the pin-pricks, the minuscule tinglings of joy in his brain. If it was real, if the seedling — whatever it was — really had sprung from those seeds . . .

Jobs didn't push away the feelings of power and pride that poured through him then. He couldn't. They were too huge and persistent. He felt like one of the famous explorers from history, like Christopher Columbus or Leif Eriksson. He was Steven

Jobs, his longtime hero, like Louis Leakey, like Galileo Galilei, all wrapped up into one. He felt, finally, like a truly important person and it made him very, very happy.

Come on, he told himself, shaking his head, embarrassed by the train of his thoughts. *Gotta figure out what to do next.*

CHAPTER TWENTY-ONE

"I'M NO HERO."

"Does this mean we're not taking off?" Roger Dodger asked.

Olga put a hand on his shoulder. "I don't know. I don't know yet what it means."

Mo'Steel eyed his best friend kneeling over that green thing and felt a frown of worry settle on his face.

"Wait here, Mom," he said.

Mo'Steel strode over to Jobs, leaned down, and took his arm. "Come on, Duck. Let the others get a look."

Jobs looked up at Mo'Steel, eyes dazed. "What? Oh, yeah."

Mo'Steel kept hold of Jobs's arm and led him off for a private talk. Jobs kept looking over his shoulder at the little green thing.

"Why does this mean so much to you, Duck?"

Mo'Steel asked when they'd stopped walking. "I mean, I'm no scientist, and no disrespect or anything, but that thing, that sprout or whatever it is, looks mighty insignificant to me. It's not like a whole field of veggies sprang up overnight or anything. We're not going to make a killing in the produce business."

"Don't you see, Mo?" Jobs said in an urgent whisper. "I feel responsible for dragging everybody to Earth in the first place. Maybe I can make up for it by really finding a way to peace. If I can convince the Troika and the Meanies and the Riders that a life on Earth really is possible for us — if I can *make* life possible for us! — then maybe we can make a deal to return Mother to them as soon as we've established a base. Maybe we finally can be free of them, and they finally can be free of us. Isn't that what everyone wants?"

Mo'Steel shrugged. "Sure, Jobs. I guess so."

"I *know* so," Jobs insisted. "Just go tell 2Face and Billy right away. You and Tate. The rest of us will stay here for a bit, see if we find anything else and *build* some sort of shelter around the seedling. Tell 2Face that when we get back on board I want an emergency meeting."

Mo'Steel hesitated. Personally, he thought Jobs

was setting himself up for a major fall. Even if that little green thing was really alive, you weren't going to jump from that to a forest in the next year, so what were you supposed to do in the meantime? And — well, Mo'Steel could see another problem, a big one. If the ash was toxic, if it resisted Jobs's efforts to purify it, how could you grow anything edible in it? But nobody was asking his opinion so he didn't offer it. Besides, Jobs was the kind of guy who'd probably thought through every possible scenario already and come up with a plan.

"Okay," Mo'Steel said. He looked at his best friend's bright but serious face and clapped a hand on Jobs's shoulder. "See you back on board."

2Face observed Mo'Steel's and Tate's faces closely. They looked sincere; 2Face was sure they weren't lying about having discovered a seedling on the surface. Still, she didn't like something about what she'd heard. It smelled of a trap — suddenly, just before takeoff, a sign of life? — but she couldn't see why it would be a trap or who would have set it. Maybe worse, if it wasn't a trap and that annoying little twit Jobs's find was for real . . . She wanted to see it for herself. There might be some way to steal the thunder, take control of the situation, make it seem that all along it was she, 2Face, who'd orchestrated the expeditions, the find, the success.

"We're going to the surface," she announced. "I want to see this miracle for myself. Then we'll decide if it's worth our staying on Earth a bit longer."

"No!" Billy said loudly.

"It's not a problem, Billy," 2Face said sternly.

"If Billy really doesn't want to go, I'll stay here with him," Mo'Steel offered. "I've seen the — whatever it is."

"Or I could stay," Tate offered.

"No," 2Face said definitively. She was not leaving Billy behind. Not even with Mo'Steel. Definitely not with Tate. The freak might try to eat him or something. "Billy," she said, "you'll come with us. It'll be okay, I promise. We'll set up that new automatic shielding device you and Jobs designed so no one can breach the bridge. All right?"

"It's dangerous," Billy said firmly. "I'm staying here. I don't want to leave Mother alone."

"But Billy," 2Face said, working to keep her voice calm, her tone reasonable, "you are Mother and Mother is you. Wherever you are she is, you know that. What does it matter if you're on or off the ship?"

Billy shook his head. "No. You go ahead. I'll wait here."

2Face shot a look at Mo'Steel, said, "Give us a minute," and pulled Billy off to the far corner of the bridge.

Mo'Steel looked at Tate. She looked as uncomfortable as he felt. "Maybe she should just, you know, leave him alone," he whispered.

Tate glanced at 2Face, then looked back at Mo'Steel. "Never happen," she whispered back.

Mo'Steel started tapping his foot, swinging his arms, humming. "What's taking her so long?" he said.

Tate shook her head. "Coercion of an innocent by a bully isn't as easy as it seems," she said bitterly.

Finally, after a full ten minutes, 2Face and Billy rejoined them. Billy looked suddenly exhausted, defeated in a way that made Mo'Steel think of an old loyal dog who's just been kicked for no reason by its longtime master.

It made Mo'Steel mad, but, hey. It was Billy's life, not his.

"I'll contact the Troika and the Meanies," 2Face said firmly. "Billy, get that new shielding device in place. Tell Tate what to do if anyone tries to come through it. Walk her through all the protocols. Mo'Steel, just wait here. We'll be ready to go soon. You can show us the way."

"What about Yago?" Mo'Steel asked. "Shouldn't we get him to come along?"

2Face laughed. "Why? All he does anymore is mumble to himself. He wouldn't know what he was looking at. No, just leave him on board."

Mo'Steel shook his head. "I'm not comfortable with that," he said.

2Face sighed. "Okay, all right. I'll put him in the guys' sleeping area."

"I'll make sure he doesn't cause trouble," Tate promised.

Mo'Steel knew when to give up. "Okay," he answered to Tate. "But be careful, okay?"

"I will," Tate promised. "I'm no hero."

Mo'Steel smiled. "Now that's what I like to hear. We'll be back soon."

Tate stood on the bridge, alone. She flashed on the big fight Tamara and Mo'Steel had had up here, back when the Baby/Shipwright had controlled Tamara like a puppet, and felt sadness overcome her. Tamara'd let Tate be nice to her but Tamara had never seemed to be able to care.

Tate tried to shake off the memories but it was no good. Suddenly, she felt as if she was being watched. No, she knew she was being watched and it gave her the heebie-jeebies. This was why back on Earth before the Rock she never went to horror movies. Too sensitive. *Careful,* she warned herself. *Don't go Mouth until you know it's the enemy.*

Slowly, Tate turned to face the door.

There, in the gloom of the immense doorway, a darker shadow . . . Still, silent, watching her. Tate felt her stomach clench.

It was Yago. And in that split second, Tate knew.

CHAPTER TWENTY-TWO

"IT'S TOO LATE."

"The Troika are sending Duncan," 2Face said. "The Meanies are sending a representative from the Quorum, probably one of the Sentients."

Jobs didn't seem to have heard. He was kneeling on the ashy ground, peering at the spindly little green thing.

"He's like Charlie Brown with that skinny Christmas tree," 2Face said to no one.

"Why did you tell the Meanies and the Troika about the seedling?" Violet challenged. "We don't know anything for sure yet."

2Face ignored her. "How you doing, Billy?" she asked. The poor kid looked like he was about to slip back into the catatonic trance they'd found him in back on the *Mayflower*. Or — like he was seriously ticked. 2Face's bravado faltered for a moment.

Billy didn't answer. Just looked at her unblinkingly, with his big dark eyes.

2Face sighed. "Why don't you go stand with Olga? Mrs. Gonzalez. Okay?" 2Face gave Billy a gentle push, watched as he glared at her before walking toward Mo'Steel's mother.

Mothers know how to deal with kids like him, 2Face thought. *I don't have time right now.*

"Here they come now," Roger Dodger called.

"Are they Yago's?" 2Face asked suspiciously.

Anamull shrugged. "They all look the same to me."

"One is," D-Caf said. "I can tell. His name is Yago's Formidable Intellect. The others, no, not Yago's."

2Face felt momentarily uneasy. She'd suggested one representative of the Children. Now she counted four Meanies and two Riders approaching. The Riders rode their hoverboards; the Meanies flew close to the ground in their blue-black suits. 2Face couldn't make out all the details from this distance but she had no doubt every one of them was armed. They were warriors, after all.

"Did we really need to have Riders here?" Olga grumbled.

"Obviously the Meanies think so," 2Face snapped.

The delegation of alien representatives got closer

and landed about three yards from the rough circle of Remnants. 2Face wondered if there was any way to get them to disarm for the duration of Jobs's little show, then gave up the notion as silly.

"We hope you have come to talk and not fight," 2Face called loudly. "We asked you here to witness an amazing discovery, one that will bring peace to us all, a discovery that will —"

"What the . . ."

2Face felt the ground beneath her rumble and for a split second thought, *Oh, no, no, no, please,* but no pillar of flame rose beneath her feet. Watching with disbelief that became horror that became disbelief again . . . 2Face watched as Mother shook off her mooring, as engines began to fire, as everyone around her stared or . . .

"No!" 2Face screamed. "No!"

"Billy!" Olga saw his eyes roll back in his head, saw his shoulders sag, saw his knees begin to buckle. She rushed forward and eased his deadweight to the ground. "He's fainted," she said, and cradled his head in her lap.

"His connection to Mother, to the ship," Violet said hurriedly. "I think it's been severed!"

D-Caf grabbed Violet's arm. "Is he going to die?"

A cry of anguish prevented Violet from responding.

"No!" 2Face started for the ship.

Mo'Steel grabbed her arm, spun her around. She shrieked and struggled. "Let me go!"

"It's too late," Mo'Steel hissed right into her face. "It's too late."

Tears streaked 2Face's cheeks. "I was so stupid! I thought he wasn't a threat anymore. Stupid!"

"Yago," Jobs whispered. And then it all became clear. Part of it, anyway. He'd been tricked. They all had. Jobs threw himself to the ground, stared hard at the seedling, then with a cry of anguish, he ripped it from the ash. There were no roots. But it had looked so real! Felt so real. An excellent fake.

Could Yago have accomplished this scheme by himself? Jobs gripped the phony seedling and thought. No. Yago had had help. It had to be the Troika. He was in league with the Troika. And the Meanies? Riders? Maybe. Maybe not. Because the stranded Meanies and Riders were clearly angry. Though maybe even that was an act. Or maybe their people had fooled them, like Yago had fooled Jobs.

Didn't matter. They were all well and royally screwed over.

They were stranded. Castaways. They had only a little food, a little water. A few weapons. The clothes on their backs. A few lead-lined bags, small shovels, and brushes and rope, a few flashlights. And one another.

Jobs wasn't so sure that was even a good thing. Because there'd been a lot of blame tossed around recently, open animosity. It had been bad enough waking aboard the *Mayflower*, realizing they were a group of mourning strangers, homeless, without food or shelter, abandoned in an alien environment. But it was worse now, yes, much worse, Jobs thought. Because now they knew what to expect from one another and it was not always comfort and support.

Jobs surveyed the sorry group.

2Face's rage had burned out. Or had seemed to. Jobs had no doubt it was still simmering just under the surface. But now she sat quietly with Billy; he was still unconscious.

Noyze wept. Violet looked blank. D-Caf, Roger Dodger, and Anamull stood openmouthed, disbelieving, staring up at the massive rising ship. Olga gripped Mo'Steel's arm, her other hand over her mouth. Ash dusted his black hair, making him look like an old man.

Tate was on the ship. Jobs hoped she'd be all

right. *Too bad we interfered when she attacked Yago,* he thought. Ironic. Tate had known back then, even if she hadn't understood.

"We've got to take them out!" Anamull barked.

Mo'Steel whirled to see the four stranded Meanies and two stranded Riders slowly drawing weapons, aiming, not shooting — not yet.

Mo'Steel's mouth went dry. "Let them make the first move, 'migo," he told Anamull. Carefully, he reached around for the crossbow strapped to his back. "Let them . . ."

Yago glared at Tate. The dull roar of Mother's engines was like sweet music to his ears.

"Not going to try to attack me?" he taunted.

Tate glared back but Yago knew she knew she was defeated.

"You can leave now," he said. A giggle escaped and Yago put a hand to his mouth in mock embarrassment.

He stood aside as Tate walked slowly from the bridge, her eyes now downcast.

When she had gone, Yago fell to his knees with laughter.

CHAPTER TWENTY-THREE

SHE WOULD WAIT.

She was called Echo.

She watched and she listened. She waited.

From deep below the surface Echo and the Alpha colony observed.

Humans. Humans with a spacecraft. It was fascinating.

The spacecraft had gone. The humans had remained.

Echo wondered.

The humans were fascinating.

Echo would watch. She would wait.

K.A. APPLEGATE

REMNANTS™

Dream Storm

"LET'S RIDE."

"I look ridiculous," Jobs complained. "Worse, I *feel* ridiculous."

"Strap it up, Duck," Mo'Steel said. "You're styling."

Jobs looked down at himself doubtfully. His legs were shoved into the rear leg holes of one of the Meanies' suits. The front leg holes hung empty because his fingers were crammed into the part of the suit designed to hold the Meanies' tentacles. This was extremely uncomfortable, but it was the only way to work the controls.

His head was also covered by the suit — which made it difficult to talk. That was fine with Jobs. He'd already said good-bye to Edward. Now he wanted to go before Violet came over. Looking out of the oversized eye holes, Jobs could see that she was standing, naturally, with D-Caf. Everyone was there — everyone but Anamull — huddled at the top of a broken stair, waiting for Jobs and Mo'Steel to fly off on their desperate mission.

"Let me help you," Noyze said, leaving Mo'Steel's side and approaching Jobs. She started fiddling with the seam that held Jobs's suit closed, sealing it up. "Maybe this will help keep you warm in the Dark Zone."

"Maybe it will keep this stupid thing from falling off," Jobs muttered nervously. He hadn't known the seam was open. Oh god — what other detail had he overlooked? Was he about to die because he had forgotten something stupid and obvious?

He noted with some surprise that he felt like throwing up. He was sweating. His hands were shaking. Being this disturbed disturbed him. He tried to take deep breaths, tried to calm himself down. Flying this crazy thing with his nerves so raw would be impossible. Deep breath in. Deep breath out.

"Let's ride," Mo'Steel said.

Jobs felt his stomach do a slow roll. "Ready." A pause. "You first."

Mo'Steel didn't hesitate. His suit suddenly shot

into the air like an overgrown bottle rocket. Thirty feet — straight up. And it kept climbing.

"Woolly!" Mo'Steel's excited voice sounded very, very far away.

Jobs heaved, choked down the bile rising from his gut and reached for a tiny button near his sweaty right ring finger.

Jobs was just slow enough for Mo'Steel to get impatient.

Time to see what this baby can do, he thought giddily. He pressed the tiny button that sent him soaring straight up into the air, and kept pressing. The Meanie rockets responded with a gigantic burst of acceleration.

Mo'Steel shot up so fast his stomach dropped to his feet. He could almost feel the adrenaline rushing into his veins and he laughed out loud. He hadn't been this happy since — well, for a long time.

He held his finger steady. Quickly, surprisingly quickly, the faces looking up at him from the ground dissolved into blurry specks.

"Mo!" Jobs yelled angrily. "Mo, you idiot, come back!"

Mo'Steel left his finger where it was and Jobs's voice was almost instantly blotted out by distance.

He was high now. Very high. He thought he could almost see the edge of the Dark Zone. Could he go high enough to get out of the dust? Could he go right into space? Mo'Steel considered trying it just to see what would happen. He was sure the suit would be fine. One small problem: he didn't have any oxygen.

No oxygen in space would not be pretty. Mo'Steel knew how it would go: First he'd start to feel dizzy. Then he'd black out and his cold finger would slide off the button. Old man g would snag him —

Without warning, Mo'Steel flipped from *imagining* himself fall to *seeing* himself fall — it was the difference between watching a movie and being one of the characters.

In perfect, horrifying detail, he saw the ground rushing up, felt dusty air pricking at his eyes and making them water, heard wind roaring in his ears. He was picking up speed, picking up speed, picking up speed, peeing his pants, letting his bowels go, kicking in panic as the distance vanished, arms windmilling, screaming and —

Thud. Hitting the ground and knowing the pain for an excruciating second before everything went misty red and then black. . . .